always mackenzie

KATE CONSTABLE

ALLEN&UNWIN

Allen & Unwin
83 Alexander St
Crows Nest NSW 2065
Australia
Phone: (61 2) 8425 0100
Fax: (61 2) 9906 2218
Email: info@allenandunwin.com
Web: www.allenandunwin.com

ISBN 978 1 74237 766 7

Design based on cover design by Tabitha King and Kirby Stalgis
Text design by Kirby Stalgis
Set in 12.5 pt Spectrum MT by Midland Typesetters, Australia
Printed in China at Everbest Printing Co.

10 9 8 7 6 5 4 3 2 1

february

'We're doomed.' Bec dumped her bags beneath the grimy window of the converted shearers shed. 'We're all going to die.'

'Doomed to death?' said Iris. 'That's got to be a tautology.'

'We won't *die*,' said Georgia. 'You never know, it might even be fun.'

I said, 'Can I have the top bunk?'

So what did that say about me?

On the flimsy evidence available, it might seem that I was a practical, confident, brisk kind of person who'd rather get on with things than stand around arguing.

Wrong, wrong, wrong and wrong again, which shows how inaccurate first impressions can be. Because standing around arguing was almost my favourite activity; I wasn't practical (I couldn't do anything with my hands), or

1

confident (I tended to be anxious and self-deprecating), or brisk (I was more of a cautious perfectionist).

Bec's comment was true to form, though. She was a pessimist: a tiny, sharp-tongued, pointy-nosed, deeply cynical person, like an impatient little bandicoot. Iris *was* pedantic about language, and a thousand other things. She was an absolute nerd, and since we shared some of the same obsessions, that made me a nerd, too. And Georgia was a simple, happy soul who liked peace and harmony and tended to look on the bright side. Bec Patel, Iris Kwong and Georgia Harris — a pessimist, a pedant and a peace-maker: my three closest friends. And me — Jem. Actually I was a Jessica, but there were so many other Jessicas and Jesses around, I became Jess M at creche, and that was shortened to Jem, so I was Jem, even at home. The M was for Martinic.

I always liked being Jem. It was a tough kind of name. A girl called Jem could become a knight and ride off on crusades, or a guitarist in a punk band, or an adventurer, trekking across Outer Mongolia on a motorbike, or sailing solo round the world. Not that I'd ever had any desire to do those things, but it was good to know that if I did decide to, my name wouldn't hold me back.

It was ironic that I had ended up with a tough name though, because I wasn't tough at all. I was one of those people who never got noticed: the Invisible Girl. Which suited me fine, most of the time. I didn't play an instrument (so much for the punk band), I wasn't into drama (I'd rather watch than perform), and I was definitely not sporty (no trekking and sailing for me). And at my school, unless you were a star at one of those activities, you were invisible.

Luckily for me there were a few of us who fell into that category. Back in Year 7, in the first few weeks of school, there was a tremendous jostling as all the girls who were going to be popular, the golden girls, arranged themselves together like those magnet stick-and-ball sets: snap! snap! snap! the musos, the drama queens, the sporting heroes. The rest of us were shunted to the edges – the rejects, the geeks, the nerds, the ugly ones, the brains. Then it was our turn to mill about until we established our own groups, huddling invisibly together in the shadow of the glowing golden ones as they sashayed about, totally oblivious to us.

That was the way it had been ever since. And that was the way it was always going to be – until Year 10 camp. For the first term of Year 10, the whole year level got bussed to the school's property on the Heathersett River. It was a tradition. And it was real back-to-nature stuff: no mobile phone signal, no internet, not even TV. We slept in old shearers sheds, and there was a roster for cooking, and we did 'challenging' activities: rafting and abseiling and camping out overnight.

I said 'challenging' like that, not because I didn't find it challenging (I certainly felt challenged; challenged out of my skin), but because that was the kind of language everyone used at Heathersett River. It was all 'getting out of your comfort zone' and 'accessing your inner resources' and 'enhancing your leadership qualities.' We were supposed to be the leaders of the future, you see; that was the motto on our school's publicity material. The first female Head of Treasury was one of our Old Girls; so was that doctor who was on the news all the time, fighting AIDS in Africa and arguing with the UN.

Everyone there was more or less smart; if you weren't, they'd weed you out before you made it as far as Heathersett River. So when I was talking about the brains before, I meant the ones who were nothing but brainy. No dazzling extras. Not brainy *and* musical; not brainy *and* sporty; not brainy *and* talented performers. Just brainy and boring. We were a bit of a disappointment; we didn't 'add value'. We just kept our heads down, held the academic success rate steady, and stayed invisible.

Actually it was slightly weird, because Georgia was a good swimmer, and Iris played a mean violin, and Bec performed in her House play last year, and she was hilarious. I was the only one who was a complete dead loss. I was the original Plain Jane, nose-in-a-book. The others glittered slightly, in the right light, but they were not quite golden. And I dragged the whole gang down. No glitter here, not even a pinch of gold dust. Which, in a perverse way, I was proud of. It was a distinction to be undistinguished in such distinguished company.

Did I mention — did I *need* to mention? — how much we'd been dreading Heathersett River? Cut off from civilisation for nine whole weeks? Marooned with the shining ones, with only the staff to break the monotony? And we each had our individual reasons for dreading it, as well.

Georgia was going to miss her mum. They're a single-parent family and they'd never been apart even for one night. Iris was addicted to *Starfield 5*, and the new series was due to start right in the middle of the Heathersett term. (Now *that* was nerdy; I quite liked *Starfield 5*, but I wasn't that bad.) Bec's brother was returning from a year in India. After a huge amount of begging and pleading and letter-writing and special meetings, she'd been given leave for *one* weekend to see him. They were pretty strict about the Heathersett River experience.

The idea was to be totally immersed, and to come out the other side a different person. I didn't like the sound of that. A proud glitter-free nerd, I was pretty comfortable with myself the way I was, thanks.

But *my* particular reason for dreading the camp was books. Reading was not one of the activities encouraged at Heathersett River. We were supposed to 'get in touch with our physical selves' and 'learn to live in our bodies.' Pure jargon and, as Iris pointed out, utterly meaningless. Where else were we going to live? The age of brains floating in glass jars or wired up to androids had not yet arrived, though Iris was looking forward to it.

Anyway, the whole point of the camp was that we spent nine weeks communing with nature and doing extreme sports before we had to think about Year 11 and 12 and uni entrance scores and all the stuff that would loom up at us like a tidal wave as soon as we returned to the real world.

So – no books. They figured we were going to spend the next two and a half years up to our eyeballs in books and study, so we should take a break while we could. But I was the kind of person who had a panic attack at the prospect of going nine *minutes* without something to read, let alone nine weeks.

Generally speaking, I was a very law-abiding person. But I seriously could not face the thought of enduring all that time without books. So I smuggled some in. Only two. Two! As if two books would be enough to last me nine weeks. But it was better than nothing. Actually one of them was four novels in one volume, in really tiny print: *The Once and Future King* by T.H. White – a great tragic romance about King Arthur, and worth reading several times, as well as being good value in words per kilo. And the other book was *Busman's Honeymoon* by Dorothy L. Sayers, because Iris and I had a crush on Lord Peter Wimsey, who was wealthy and witty and swanned around solving crimes in the 1930s. I knew Iris would read it, too. She had her heart set on going to Oxford University in England – I suspected because she thought she'd meet her own Peter Wimsey there. I said I'd go, too. Nothing to do with Wimsey, of course.

It was *Busman's Honeymoon* that got me into trouble. It was a hardback, and difficult to hide. On the second day at Heathersett River, Mrs Peterson – I mean 'Fiona', we had to call staff by their first names while we were away – saw it sticking out from under my pillow, and promptly confiscated it.

'Any more?' she said. A maths teacher, she might have let me keep *The Joy of Fractals*, but she wasn't sympathetic to novel-addiction. Mrs Renton (aka Danielle) might have turned a blind eye.

As I said, I was a law-abiding person, so I gave up the T.H. White as well. Can you imagine my pain at losing those books? I actually cried.

I guess it wasn't just the books. I was missing Mum and Dad, and I was struggling with being so far out of my comfort zone. Lukewarm two-minute showers; the flies; bunk beds; food that was either burnt or undercooked, because we weren't the most experienced chefs and none of us had figured out how to cook for eighty people. Even the toilet facilities were only just adequate.

And I was an only child. I used to wish I had brothers and sisters to share things with, to play with. But as Mum pointed out, if I actually had siblings they'd probably drive me crazy. I liked things to stay where I'd put them; I liked it that I could open the door of my room and find everything exactly where I'd left it. Poor Iris had a younger brother and he spent his life finding ways to wreck hers.

As much as I loved Bec and Iris and Georgia, I wasn't used to sharing a room with anyone, let alone with one person who *always* left her towel on the floor (Georgia), one person who picked her nose (sorry, Iris) and one who borrowed other people's clothes without asking – even underwear – when she'd forgotten to wash her own (that really irked me, Bec).

Not that I was perfect. Obsessive neatness might be annoying if you're not naturally neat yourself. It took me a while to realise that the others were getting irritated when I tidied up – I mean, who wouldn't rather live in a neat, organised room (or shearers shed), than a squalid one? Well, the answer to that was, apparently, my three friends.

So what with one thing and another, none of us were feeling very happy. It was weird. Heathersett River *was* life-changing, and I didn't even see it coming.

Oddly enough, it was Bec who started it. For some reason, Bec got it into her head that she wanted to go horse riding.

It was clear from the first day that certain activities were reserved for certain (golden) people. Not officially, of course. Officially, we all had to try everything at least once, and then we were encouraged to concentrate on only a couple of activities to 'develop our skills and competencies' and 'enhance our confidence and leadership potential'. Which meant that non-shiny people ended up with the lame, low-glamour activities, such as fishing, art (i.e. gluing rocks together to express our emotions about the land) and bushwalking, while the golden types — Mackenzie Woodrow and Jessica Samuels and their gangs — spent their days horse riding and rock climbing and whitewater rafting.

As I said, this was very clear. Clear to everyone except Bec Patel. Bec could be funny like that; sometimes she just didn't get it. She came across as this jaded, knowing person, but she could be quite naive about the way the world worked: our world, anyway. Iris and I actually had to sit her down in Year 8 and explain about the golden girls, and she genuinely didn't believe us. She still asked us, sometimes, who was who. She didn't see the trip-wires everyone else carefully stepped over. Of course, sometimes she stumbled over them herself, like with the horse riding, but she didn't understand *why* she suddenly landed face-first in the dirt. That was why she tried out for the House play; she honestly didn't realise that only golden girls got parts. But she was so amazingly funny that they *had* to give it to her, and then she thought she'd proved that Iris and I were just paranoid, because we'd said it was impossible.

By the third week, we'd all tried every activity at least once, and we were settling into our special areas. Then at dinner Bec announced she wanted to go horse riding again. Georgia and Iris and I stared at her as if she were crazy. We wondered if her weekend in the outside world, seeing her brother, had temporarily blinded her to the Heathersett River rules. But then we realised she was just being Bec.

'But Mackenzie and Philippa and Rosie Lee are horse riding tomorrow,' said Georgia. 'I heard them talking about it in the shower block.'

'There might be a space for me,' said Bec. 'I'll check.'

She scribbled her name on the horse-riding list and came back to our table looking very pleased with herself.

'I told you there'd be room.'

'You don't understand,' said Iris. 'You're upsetting the delicate balance of nature. Was Frances on the list?'

'No.'

'Late as usual. So she'll have to join the rafting group instead. Which will push Jasmin into abseiling. Which will push Sam into hiking. It's called the domino effect.'

'And Jess Casinader will end up fishing with us,' I said.

'I like Jess Casinader,' said Georgia.

'That's not the point,' said Iris. 'The point is, it's a chain reaction. There could be a complete meltdown.'

Iris was planning a career in nuclear physics.

'I don't care,' said Bec. 'I want to go horse riding. It's not fair.'

We were sure Bec would end up as some kind of activist. I could just imagine her being dragged away by the cops, sticking out her sharp little chin and squeaking, 'Why are you arresting me? It's just not fair.'

Really, Georgia should have been the one demanding more contact with animals. She wanted to be a vet. But she never made a fuss about anything.

Next day, sure enough, all hell broke loose.

There was a domino effect, though the dominoes didn't fall exactly as Iris and I predicted. We ended up with Sara-Grace Fratelli in our fishing group, not Jess Casinader, but the effect of the effect was the same – the camp was full of grumbling and aggrieved looks and girls muttering, 'It wasn't *my* fault.' It was so bad, even the staff noticed, and though the normal policy was to let us sort out our own problems, the counsellor – 'Trish' – decided that we needed a sharing session.

It was hideous. We'd already had a couple of sharing sessions, the first one when we'd arrived and worked out what the camp rules were going to be. Supposedly we students decided the rules so we would 'own' them, but I'm pretty sure our final list matched one the Head had given to Trish before we left. Iris suggested a rule of 'no more sharing sessions', but Trish didn't put that one up for debate.

And then we had a session of trust exercises and medi-ation, and boy, how we wished we'd backed up Iris.

Before the trust sharing session we pushed aside the

tables in the dining shed and arranged the chairs in a circle. The staff leaned against the walls and looked grumpy. I guess it wasn't much fun for them, either, being stuck in the bush for nine weeks with us while we 'learned to live in our bodies'.

Trish made us all number off, one to ten, then all the Ones had to join up together and all the Twos and so on. So there were ten groups of five or six girls and all the normal friendship gangs were broken up. I was with Mackenzie Woodrow and Jessica Harper and Sara-Grace Fratelli and a funny little girl called Sonia Darcy who was about two years younger than the rest of us and some kind of IT child prodigy.

I'd never spoken to Mackenzie Woodrow in my life. Sara-Grace Fratelli and Jessica Harper used to be best friends, but they'd had a huge falling out last year and since then they'd hated each other. They glared at each other across our little ring of chairs. Sonia gazed into space, lips moving, probably dreaming up some new hacker code.

Mackenzie muttered, '*This* is going to be fun.' I nearly laughed, but I didn't dare. She wasn't talking to me; Mackenzie Woodrow glittered so brightly beyond my orbit, like a comet blazing overhead, that I could only glance at her briefly in case my eyes were blinded by her radiance. She *looked* golden. She had blonde hair, beautifully cut, that swung around her face like a bell, and big blue eyes, and killer cheekbones. She was no dumb blonde, though; she was sporty *and* into drama *and* brainy, the triple whammy. Everyone knew she was going to be an actress — a brilliant one. She even looked like Cate Blanchett.

Trish said she had figured out that existing 'friendship groups' were at the bottom of all the trouble. Mackenzie didn't say *well, der*, but the expression on her face was so eloquent that again I had to bite back a laugh.

We were issued with textas and butcher's paper and instructed to brainstorm how we felt about the groups. All around the room I saw blank faces. Sara-Grace and Jessica turned their backs to each other, and Sonia just blinked. 'What groups?' She was even more of an innocent than Bec, who'd got us into this mess in the first place.

'It's up to us, Jen,' said Mackenzie, and she seized the textas and flopped down on the floor. She even flopped gracefully, tucking her hair behind her ear and somehow arranging herself as she went down. I wasn't surprised that she'd got my name wrong, she was such a long way above my orbit, and anyway, I was invisible. And I wasn't surprised she'd grabbed the textas. That was simply her way of exercising her leadership qualities.

And when I saw what she was writing, it confirmed everything I'd suspected about her.

<u>Nerds</u>   • act superior
              • show off in class
              • try to make the rest of us feel stupid

I said, 'What are you talking about?'

She gave me a long, cool, blue stare. 'You know what I mean. You're one of them.' She leaned over and her hair swung in front of her perfect cheekbones as she wrote.

<u>Musos</u>
- cliquey
- speak in language we can't understand
- injure us with hard instrument cases on bus

Well, *that* was true. Music School girls always droned on about minims and crotchets and A minor chords. Music was a Big Deal at our school; we held three concerts a year, one at the Arts Centre in the city, like professionals. Professional standards were expected, and the muso students acted like professional prima donnas. The musos were even allowed to bring their instruments to camp so they could practise. Miss Macmillan, the Head of Music, insisted. Which was, as Bec would say, so unfair.

Mackenzie obviously didn't have much time for musos. I would have laughed if I hadn't been so furious about what she'd written about the 'nerds'. We could call ourselves that, but coming from a golden girl, it was definitely an insult.

Sara-Grace was a muso (clarinet) and she cast Mackenzie a look that could kill. 'May I have the pen, please?'

Mackenzie smiled and handed it over, and Sara-Grace scrawled:

14

<u>Athletes</u> · think their sexier/skinnier than us
· ARE sexier/skinnier than us,
because they starve themselves

Sara-Grace refolded her arms as if to say, my work here is done. Did I mention that Mackenzie was sporty as well as an actress? She was in the top tennis team, and I mean the top team, with the Year 12s. She read what Sara-Grace had written and spread her hands helplessly. So she was skinny, and sexy. Mackenzie Woodrow wasn't even going to try to deny it.

I could have taken the pen and corrected Sara-Grace's spelling of *their* to *they're* but that would have proved Mackenzie's point, so I didn't. It made my fingers itch, though, so I sat on my hands. But then Mackenzie gave me that cool, smug, Oscar-winning smile, and I knew that she knew that Sara Grace's *their* was killing me.

Jessica Harper hadn't chipped in yet. She was sporty too, an all-round star. I couldn't remember what she was good at. Hurdles maybe, and discus, and long jump or something? I didn't pay much attention. Anyway she was absolutely a golden girl, though she and Mackenzie were in different gangs, and she was pretty sexy too, in a lean, brunette kind of way. She glared at Sara-Grace and Mackenzie and held out her hand for the pen, and wrote:

<u>Drama queens</u> · up themselves
· bimbos
· weird

Then she sat back and folded *her* arms.

'That's raised the tone of the debate,' I said. 'I thought we nerds had the monopoly on weird.'

'You're not weird,' drawled Mackenzie. 'You're not *interesting* enough to be weird.'

Sara-Grace and Jessica laughed. That summed it all up. The shiny people might have their own sub-tribes, their own petty feuds, but when the chips hit the fan (as my nana would say), they'd unite in a nanosecond to humiliate the rest of us. The grand old alliance of the golden would always triumph. I looked away. Why should I care what Mackenzie Woodrow said to raise a laugh from her minions?

Sonia Darcy was staring at us wide-eyed. She said plaintively, 'Are you talking about different groups at school? Like the houses in *Harry Potter*?'

'Yes, honey,' said Mackenzie soothingly.

'Which one am I?'

'You're a nerd, sweetie. Like Jen here.'

'But I'm not even friends with Jem.' Sonia eyed me with mild distaste. 'She doesn't know *anything*.' She meant I didn't know anything about computers. Well, it wasn't compulsory. I might have been a nerd, but I wasn't a geek.

I stood up. 'This whole session is an exercise in futility. I'm leaving.'

Mackenzie raised a perfect eyebrow. 'I think you'll find that trying to leave is an exercise in futility.'

She was right. I was completely hemmed in by clusters of chairs; girls were bent earnestly over butcher's paper, deep in conversation. And then I realised: girls were *crying*.

I sank back in my chair, stunned. Then I scanned the room for my own tribe. Georgia was in a corner, wiping her eyes, talking to *Rosie Lee*. The same Rosie Lee who wouldn't (as my nana would say) pee on one of us if we were on fire. Bec had disappeared. Maybe she'd managed to escape. But there was Iris – Iris Kwong, my so-called best friend, who I was supposed to go to Oxford with one day, and she was *hugging* Jasmin Hussan.

'I hope someone gets a photo,' said Mackenzie, following the direction of my gaze. 'What a perfect shot for the cultural diversity section of the school prospectus.'

'Oh, shut up,' I snapped wittily. At that point, my flabber was totally gasted. I'd just seen Bec come back in, with Phillipa and Frances, and they'd clearly all been crying. Bec *never* cries. She didn't even cry when she got a B for one story in her creative composition project in Year 7 English, and she always said that was the worst thing that had ever happened to her . . .

Mackenzie Woodrow was an island of relative sanity in the dining shed, the only other person who wasn't in tears. Even Sara-Grace and Jessica Harper were misty-eyed. Mackenzie and I looked at each other, and I could see she was as appalled as I was.

'This is ridiculous,' she said.

'Ludicrous,' I agreed.

'It's worse than a Charles Le Tan workshop.'

'Pardon?'

Mackenzie rolled her eyes. 'You've never heard of Charles Le Tan? He's "inspirational".' She made quote marks with her fingers. 'My dad's *in love* with him. He says things like *the universe throws us gifts; it's up to us to catch them.*'

I winced. 'Ouch.'

Frances's voice rose above the sound of sobs. 'I just never understood what it was like for *you*.' Bec was nodding earnestly; where was my sharp-tongued, cynical Bec? I couldn't believe this.

Mackenzie stood up. 'You're right, Jen. We've got to get out of here. This is insane.'

She picked her way through the huddles of weeping students, and because she was Mackenzie Woodrow, girls automatically moved aside to let her pass. I followed, but I had to weave around in Mackenzie's wake, darting through the gaps before they closed up again. I told you I was the Invisible Girl.

Mackenzie made a beeline for the kitchen, and we ducked out through the back door where the bins were lined up like sentinels. It stank, but it was quiet, and no one was crying.

'Did you see the staff?' said Mackenzie.

I nodded. 'They're ecstatic. It's a dream come true.'

'The whole of Year 10, bonding as one. Do you think this happens every year?'

'No way. We'd have heard about it. Someone would have warned us.'

Mackenzie peered back through the doorway. 'Now they're all swearing eternal friendship. Oh my god. Trish has got everyone in a big circle again. Oh my *god*!'

'What? What's going on?'

'Everyone's *holding hands*.'

We looked at each other in horror, and burst out laughing.

I said, 'Maybe aliens have infiltrated the camp.' Instantly I wished I hadn't; it was such a nerdy thing to say.

But Mackenzie didn't seem to care. 'Infiltrated everyone but us. We're the sole survivors, Jen.'

'It's *Jem*, actually.' I wished I hadn't said that either; another pedantic, superior correction from the nerd. But it was my name.

'Oh, sorry, really?' said Mackenzie. 'As in Jemima?'

'No, as in Jess M.'

'Oh, yeah,' said Mackenzie slowly, as if she was accessing distant memory files. 'Jess Martinic, right?' She pronounced it Martin*ick*.

'Martin*ich*.' There I went again.

But she repeated it. 'Martin*ich*. Right, sorry.'

'You know what we have to do?' I said randomly.

'What?'

'Swear eternal enmity. To balance things up. We should swear to be enemies forever.'

'I know what enmity means, Jem. I studied *Romeo and Juliet* last year too, you know.'

'Oh. Of course. Sorry.'

Mackenzie held up her hand in the light that streamed from the kitchen door. 'I swear—'

'I *solemnly* swear—'

'I solemnly swear that I will never, ever be friends with Jess Martin*ich* as long as we both shall live.'

'And I solemnly swear that I will never, ever be friends with Mackenzie Woodrow or hold hands with her or cry on her shoulder, as long as we both shall live.'

'Excellent,' said Mackenzie, and we slapped hands.

We crept around and peeped in the windows; the circle was fraying round the edges, girls were wandering off, making mugs of hot chocolate at the big urn. The staff were rapt, especially Ms Wells; she was bounding around like the Easter bunny. Then Rosie Lee turned on the stereo, and Jessica Samuels started to dance (typical), and she pulled little Sonia Darcy onto her feet, and soon the whole shed was full of girls jiggling and swaying. I was relieved to see Georgia and Iris and Bec standing awkwardly by the wall where they belonged; events hadn't got *completely* out of hand. I think if I'd seen Iris dancing that would have sent me over the edge. Iris didn't do dancing.

Mackenzie said, 'Probably safe to sneak in now.'

'No, thanks. I'm going to bed.'

'You don't want to dance?'

'Er, no. You know what they say about two left feet? I've got two left feet stuck on backwards.'

'How do you cope at the socials?'

'I never go to the socials.'

'Really? Never?'

'Really. Never.'

Mackenzie didn't say anything, but I could read her mind. *Loser, ugly, social reject,* was the gist of it.

'You're not missing much,' she said at last. 'The guys just stand around and talk about football and cricket.'

'Do they?' This was news to me; I didn't know any boys. 'Zero interest in football, but I like cricket; I could talk about cricket.'

'They don't talk about cricket to the girls. Just to each other.'

'What kind of a dumb rule is that?'

'It's not a rule. It's just what happens.'

'Like your gang taking all the horse-riding spots?'

'Kind of,' said Mackenzie after a pause. 'You want a hot chocolate?'

'No, thanks. I'm going to bed.'

'Don't forget. Enemies forever.'

'Enemies forever,' I echoed, and I walked through the dark, shaking my head. I guess she went back into the dining shed and danced; probably everyone cleared a space for her, so she could twirl and shimmy and sway like a graceful reed, or whatever it is that fabulous dancers do.

It was nice to have our shearers shed to myself, however briefly. While I got ready for bed I kept thinking how bizarre it was to have had a conversation with Mackenzie Woodrow, of all people. *When she's famous*, I thought, *I can tell my grandchildren about it*. Just another of those challenging Heathersett River experiences.

It could so easily not have happened at all. If we hadn't both been Threes, if I hadn't sat down where I did, if Bec hadn't wanted to go horse riding . . . It's scary, when you think about it. How small the chances are that change your life.

march

The afterglow of the amazing bonding session lasted for the next few days. Girls floated around, making a great show of sitting next to unlikely allies at breakfast: *Look at us! We can be friends! Even though we've got absolutely nothing in common!*

Everyone was super-nice to everyone else. Spots in the shower queue were sacrificed, compliments were exchanged, duty roster places swapped. *You'd rather sweep out the dining shed than chop carrots? No problem! You'd rather chop carrots than clean the toilet block? Er — okay . . . Sara-Grace, I'll teach you to play chess. Oh, thank you, Bec, I'll teach you to put on eye make-up.* (I'm not kidding, that actually happened. Yes, books were banned, but eye make-up was perfectly okay. How twisted was that?)

It was as though a religious conversion had swept through the whole camp and the only people left untouched were Mackenzie Woodrow and me. In the week after that first crazy, touchy-feely night, we didn't actually speak, but at least once a day we'd catch each other's eye and one of us (usually her) would wink or silently mouth *Enemies forever!* We were so proud of ourselves, relieved we hadn't bought into the whole artificial-sweetener world that Heathersett River had become.

For those few days it was really hard even to talk to Bec and Iris and Georgia. I'd assumed that they'd wake up in the morning and yawn and say, *Oh my, what a terrible dream!* But that hadn't happened. They'd all taken it seriously, especially Georgia. She'd become very matey with Rosie Lee, who'd apparently confided all kinds of dark secrets to her that night, and the two of them regularly disappeared down to the river together, allegedly to swim, but really to have long, meaningful conversations, and Georgia would come back burdened with the weight of Rosie's world. I was sure it couldn't last, because Rosie was such a wild child and Georgia was straight as they come.

It was disconcerting to see my friends under such an evil spell. I began to question my own sense of what was normal; I wondered if I was the crazy one. Seriously, if it had gone on much longer, I might have turned weird myself.

Iris was the first to crack. I knew she would be; her sense of irony was too strong to dissolve under this deluge of sugar-sweetness. I knew the evil magic was weakening the day I set off for a bushwalk and she came running after me.

'I thought you were doing tai chi with Phillipa,' I said.

'If I have to spend one more minute with Phillipa I will go insane,' said Iris, and a huge sigh of relief welled up inside me. I could have kissed her.

The others held out slightly longer, but it was no use; the tide had turned, and normality reasserted itself.

It was like *Wife Swap*. In theory the ones who swap places have their horizons broadened and learn about different philosophies of life, but usually at the end the wife runs back to her own family blubbing, *I never knew how much I loved you! That other family were FREAKS!* Not that I watch *Wife Swap*. Well, maybe once or twice.

By the end of the week, the friendship groups were back in place, more strongly cemented than ever. They'd all had a glimpse of life on the other side, and guess what? They didn't like it.

The next Saturday, a week after the touchy-feely night, I was rostered onto cooking duty. So was Mackenzie Woodrow. Now normal transmission had resumed and we didn't all have to pretend to love each other any more, there was no need to remind her that we were enemies to the death, so I just ignored her and concentrated on stirring the white sauce. And I only took my attention off it for a minute. I don't even know if curdled is the right word, that's how much I knew about cooking. But when Mackenzie materialised as I was scraping it into the bin, and laughed her charming Cate Blanchett laugh, I was ready to knock her on the head with the saucepan.

'I hate white sauce,' I said through gritted teeth as I scrubbed out the saucepan. 'White sauce is what my nana puts on fish. It makes me gag.'

'What about lasagne? I thought all you—' Mackenzie stopped, and actually blushed.

'What? You thought all nerds loved lasagne?'

'No-o. But I thought you – Italians – would eat it all the time.'

She meant wogs, but she was too polite to say so.

'I'm Croatian, actually. And no, my family aren't big on lasagne. My dad's got a thing against mince.'

'Well, we're making lasagne now,' said Mackenzie. She must have been paying more attention to the rest of the kitchen than I was. 'I'll teach you to make a *bechamel* sauce to die for.' She waltzed to the cool room, then waltzed back with her arms full of ingredients.

'The love-fest is over, remember?'

'This is nothing to do with love, Martinic. I'm showing off. This is all about making you feel *bad*.'

Phillipa gave us a look from the other side of the kitchen. I frowned back at her.

'First, the butter.' Mackenzie dropped a huge lump of butter into the saucepan and immediately it sizzled round

26

the edges. 'Next, the flour, stir it in. See how it's turned into a paste? That's called a roux.'

'I rue the day I let you take over the cooking.'

'R-O-U-X, it's French, you peasant. Cook on low heat for a couple of minutes. Then the milk.'

Jaylene, the cook (her actual title was Nutrition Manager or something), wandered over and watched for a while, but it was clear Mackenzie had everything under control so she wandered off again.

'The secret of *great* bechamel sauce,' said Mackenzie, 'is to add a *dribble* of milk. Guaranteed no lumps. Now stir that in. And a dribble more. See? Smooth as George Clooney.'

'George *Clooney*? Isn't he about a hundred and three?'

'Maybe so, but he's still smooth. You prefer someone else?'

I said nothing. I could have mentioned Lord Peter Wimsey, but she wouldn't have known who I was talking about, and anyway, he's not particularly smooth. I just kept pouring and stirring, pouring and stirring, until we had a saucepan full of creamy liquid.

'Keep stirring till it thickens. Patience, Martinic. And don't let it stick to the bottom.'

So I stirred patiently while Mackenzie darted back and forth, adding salt and white pepper and finally a shake of nutmeg. 'Of course it would be better with whole nutmegs, freshly ground, but in this place . . .'

'Peasants . . .' I didn't know there *was* such a thing as whole nutmegs. I squealed. 'It's thickening!'

Mackenzie turned off the burner and ran her finger along the wooden spoon. 'Taste that,' she commanded.

I licked her finger. 'Good.'

'Good? It's bloody fantastic. Jaylene! The bechamel sauce is ready!'

Jaylene dipped her teaspoon in Mackenzie's creation. She only grunted, but clearly it was the best white sauce she'd ever tasted, and only sensitivity toward the less gifted kitchen-helpers prevented her from turning cartwheels and whooping in delight. That was my reading of the grunt, anyway.

Mackenzie smiled her dazzling smile.

I have to say the lasagne was pretty good; I had two helpings. I caught myself keeping an eye out for Mackenzie, so I could say, *not bad*, or something equally lame, but as soon as I realised I was doing it, I stopped. She was on the other side of the dining shed anyway, with her gang, and the moment never came.

A couple of days later I went swimming with Georgia. The river was beautiful, even if it was a bit low with the drought. It was slow, and brown, yet clear, like the golden-brown glass of a beer bottle, and we could see smooth stones and sticks at the bottom. It was the kind of river I could imagine platypuses living in, though I don't know if they actually did. I wasn't a great swimmer – I'd always hated putting my head under – but I loved floating around in that brown clear water with the sun dappling through the gum trees, hearing the rapids plash upstream, and the bellbirds and pardalotes calling from the bank, and the rhythmic splashes from Georgia as she swam earnestly across the natural pool and back.

I was floating in the cool water, thinking about nothing – oh, all right, I was having the conversation with Lord Peter Wimsey where he renounces Harriet Vane because he's fallen in love with me – when a *head* shot up from the water right beside me. I shrieked, and flailed about, and swallowed about a litre of water, like an idiot.

Mackenzie Woodrow grinned and smoothed her hair. 'Rosie felt like a dip,' she said, and there was Rosie Lee's sleek black head bobbing up and down next to Georgia.

I couldn't think of anything to say. I nodded, and hoped she'd go away and leave me to my daydream.

'Bet you were surprised,' she said.

'Yeah, I nearly drowned.'

She laughed. 'I didn't mean *now*. I meant about the cooking.' She threw me a look that I couldn't interpret. I wasn't very good at reading other people's signals, maybe that's why I was a nerd.

'What about the cooking?'

'I bet you didn't expect me to be an expert in the culinary arts.'

'I hadn't really thought about it.'

She was silent a moment, as if I'd surprised *her*, and that gave me a prickle of resentment. Did she really assume that I didn't have anything better to think about than why Mackenzie Woodrow was interested in cooking? I did have a *life*. Yeah, that's why I was floating in the river having imaginary conversations with fictional characters.

She said, 'It's not very glamorous.'

'You're kidding, right? Bill Granger, Nigella, Kylie Kwong?'

'Is Iris related?'

'No. Isn't food styling the new . . .' I tried to think of something cool and glamorous, and failed. 'The new fashion?'

'Not bechamel sauce. Bechamel sauce is the old fashion.' Mackenzie dipped lower so just her enormous blue eyes were visible, very serious, above the waterline. She re-emerged to say, 'I like the old-fashioned stuff, sauces, and baking and pastry. The old-fashioned stuff takes *skill*. Anyone can throw pomegranates and seafood and fennel together, that's easy. But *dough* – that's a whole different plate of dumplings. I love to make my own bread.' She was speaking very low, intensely, as if this was a momentous secret. But I honestly couldn't see why it should be.

I said, 'Do you mean comfort food?'

'*Yes*! Yes, exactly!'

'O-kay,' I said.

'I've never told anyone this before,' she whispered. 'But I want to be a cook.'

'Not an actress?'

'Where did you get that idea?' she said sharply.

'Gee, I don't know, the fact that you've starred in every House play since Year 7? Everyone knows you're going to be an actress.'

'Actor,' she said. So she could be pedantic too. 'Well, I don't want to be an actor. Or a lawyer, or a model. I want to be a cook.'

'Okay, so be a chef. You can have your own show, you'll be Australia's Nigella. Go for it.'

'*No*. That's not what I want at all. I want to be a cook. Not a chef, definitely not a celebrity chef. A plain cook, a great cook.'

'Okay, okay!' This conversation was getting too intense for me. 'Be a cook. No one's stopping you.'

She snorted. 'Yeah? Mum's pushing me to be a model, my friends are all pressuring me to be an actor, my coach says I should concentrate on tennis, the school says, just don't limit your *options* . . . Dad would go *bananas* if I became a cook.'

At least Mackenzie *had* options. I didn't have a clue what I was going to do with my life.

I said, 'No one can make you do something you don't want to do. It's your life . . . What's your dad's problem? Was he attacked by a knife-wielding chef or something?'

Mackenzie gave me a sharp look, then she let out a huge sigh. 'No. He just wants me to be a lawyer.'

'Oh.'

We floated in silence for a minute, then Mackenzie said, 'I did know your name.'

'Huh?'

'I just pretended not to know your name. I didn't want you to think I'd been stalking you or anything.'

'Strangely enough, if you had known my name, given that we've been going to school together for the past *three years*, I wouldn't have assumed you'd been stalking me, no.' I started to wade toward the bank, but Mackenzie grabbed my arm.

'Promise you won't tell anyone about the cooking?'

'Okay, I promise.' Sheesh, did this girl think she was the centre of the universe, or what? Georgia was by the other bank, with Rosie Lee. I waved, and Rosie gave me a dark look. Who knows what they were talking about: Rosie's secret burning desire to be a dental technician, probably. I went for a shower.

But in spite of myself, I kept thinking about that conversation with Mackenzie. It seemed a bizarre secret, but bizarre or not, Mackenzie had chosen me to confide in, and I couldn't help being flattered.

Then I thought, *she clearly believes cooking is a dull and uncool occupation.* Which is why she'd chosen to tell a dull and uncool person about it, because it would seem quite normal to me. Which it did. So that made me doubly dull and uncool, didn't it?

Anyway, I didn't tell anyone. Partly because I knew Bec, Iris and Georgia wouldn't be interested, but mostly because, well, Mackenzie had trusted me. I'd promised. And I keep my promises.

My Croatian great-grandfather was a partisan in the Second World War. He kept his promises, too. He swore he'd never betray his country. There was a big meeting in the town square and he refused to salute the Nazi flag, so they shot him. His wife died not long after, when their baby was born, and so that baby, my grandfather, was raised by two aunts. He came out to Australia when he was twenty years old.

My dad was very proud of Grandpa Darko. I thought about him a lot. I wondered if I could ever be that brave, if someone waved a gun in my face; I wondered if I'd do what was right, or just do what everyone else was doing. I hoped I'd never have to choose between being safe and invisible, and standing out and getting shot for it.

Life at Heathersett River rolled along. There were more bonding activities, but the staff never managed to recapture the cathartic touchy-feely scenes of that crazy evening.

Bec and I went to dawn yoga classes, which were

peaceful and serene. Georgia and I went rafting, which was *terrible*. I've never been so scared in my life. 'Challenging' is one thing, but being swept down boiling rapids and hurled against rocks is something else *entirely*.

One afternoon I took my journal to the riverbank, and stretched out under the majestic river gums. We weren't supposed to show our journals to anyone except the staff, and when the holidays came, we were to use what we'd written to reflect on our time at camp. For assessment, naturally.

I hadn't been there long when Mackenzie Woodrow sauntered over. At first I thought she must have mistaken me for a cool person, then I wondered if she'd come to share more of her passion for nana cooking – swap recipes for trifle perhaps. She sat on the grass and stretched out her legs (long, golden, smooth). I tucked my own legs out of sight (pale, stumpy, unshaven).

'Writing your journal?'

'Reading it,' I admitted. 'Nothing else to read, and it's killing me.'

'I used to read a lot, when I was little. But I got out of the habit. Too much else to do, I guess.'

'Well, as you know,' I said dryly. 'That's not a problem for me.'

'Come on, you must have a social life. What do you do at weekends?'

'Read.'

'Ha, ha.'

The thing was, I wasn't kidding. Tragic, eh.

She said, 'What boys do you hang out with?'

'I don't know any boys.'

'Seriously? How can you not know any boys? They're everywhere, they're always underfoot – like cockroaches.' She made a dramatic gesture and we both laughed.

'Can I read your journal?'

'No way.' I sat on it, just to be on the safe side. 'If you want something to read, there are two books in the staff shed. Mine. Confiscated.'

'Wow, you smuggled books in? You rebel.'

'That's me. Living on the edge.'

'Most people had *alcohol* confiscated, or mobile phones.'

'Most people?'

'A few people.' She didn't mention Rosie; she didn't have to. She sat up straight and her eyes gleamed. 'Do you want them back?'

'I'll get them back at the end of camp. Unless there's a book-burning ceremony.'

'I mean, do you want them back *now*?'

'Well, yeah. But you can't always get what you want.'

'Martinic, if you want it badly enough, you can *always* get what you want. That's what Charles Le Tan says, so it must be true. Come on.'

Bemused, I followed her up the slope and back to camp. She marched straight to the staff shed door and knocked. There was no answer. During the day most of the staff were out and about supervising activities, so that was no great surprise. 'This way,' commanded Mackenzie, and led me round the back of the staff shed. She stopped and put her hands on the glass.

'What are you doing?'

'Trying the window.'

'Someone'll see!'

'I can't open it anyway.' She fell back.

'Okay, you tried. Let's go.' I was getting nervous.

'We're not giving up. Time for Plan B.' She marched off again, this time toward the tennis courts. Miss Marshall was there, refereeing a doubles match. She was the youngest staff member at the camp; she was probably only a few years older than we were. It was her first year teaching, and the Head had thrown her straight into Heathersett River, and she never seemed quite sure what the proper rules were for anything. Good choice, Mackenzie.

'Oh, Miss, Miss!' Mackenzie broke into a run. 'Oh, I'm so glad I found you. Mrs Renton – I mean Danielle – she sent me to fetch something from the staffroom, but she forgot to give me the key and I can't run all the way back to the bird-watching paddock, I'll *die*.'

Miss Marshall looked flustered. She felt in her pocket for the key, then she stopped. 'What is it Danielle wants you to fetch exactly?'

'Her binoculars,' said Mackenzie, not missing a beat. Yeah, terrible actress.

'I suppose I should come with you,' said Miss Marshall. The doubles match had stopped; all four players swung their racquets sulkily, waiting for her.

'Oh, yes, Miss,' said Mackenzie, apparently shocked that Miss Marshall would even consider any alternative; then Miss Marshall handed her the key. 'I know I can trust *you*, Mackenzie.' She didn't even glance at me, the Invisible Girl. 'Bring it straight back.'

Side by side Mackenzie and I ran toward the staff shed. 'I can't *believe* . . .' I gasped. 'And she *trusts* you.' I was exhilarated, but I felt a bit sick as well; I was such a law-abiding citizen. Smuggling in the books in the first place was wickedness enough to last me my whole school career.

'It's a dumb rule anyway,' said Mackenzie, cool as a cucumber, fitting the key in the lock. 'Why shouldn't you have books if you want them?'

I wasn't going to argue with that. Once we were inside I spotted the books straight away and shoved them up my shirt.

'Anything else while we're here?' Mackenzie gazed about. 'Chocolate biscuits? Bottle of vodka? Wonder who that belongs to.'

'NO!'

'You're no fun, Martinic. I'll take the key back and tell

her you're taking the binoculars to Mrs Renton. You go and hide those books, properly this time.'

I hurried away to our shed while Mackenzie sprinted back to the tennis court. She was bold, I had to give her that. I could imagine her staring down a Nazi with a gun in his hand.

That night as we were getting ready for bed, Iris spied the Dorothy Sayers book and yelped. 'Did Peterson give it back?'

'Not exactly.' I hesitated, then confessed; Mackenzie hadn't sworn me to secrecy this time. I guess I was expecting them to react to Mackenzie's daring the same way I had, with slightly horrified, grudging admiration. What I didn't expect was cold silence.

'Be careful, Jem,' said Iris eventually.

'No one saw us. Mrs Peterson's probably forgotten she ever confiscated the books; she won't notice they're gone.'

'I don't mean that. I mean you should be careful of Mackenzie Woodrow.'

'What?' I said. 'Why?'

'She's using you, Jem,' piped up Bec.

'Using me? For what?'

'We haven't figured that out yet.' Georgia rolled over in her bunk.

'What do you mean, *we*?' Had they been discussing me behind my back? 'So what about Rosie Lee?' My voice was squeaky. 'Is she *using* you?'

'Rosie Lee's all right,' said Georgia. 'She just needs someone to talk to.'

'Someone who isn't *superficial*, like her other friends,' said Iris pointedly.

I opened my mouth and closed it again.

'Don't tell me Mackenzie Woodrow needs someone to talk to,' said Bec.

'For Pete's sake,' I said finally, which was Iris's and my pet phrase. 'We've only spoken to each other about twice. It's not like she wants to be my *friend*.'

'We didn't think you cared about hanging out with the cool group,' said Iris.

'I *don't*!'

'Just be careful, that's all,' said Bec. 'We're only saying this because we're worried about you. We don't want you to get hurt.'

'Thanks,' I said. 'Thanks very much.' I climbed into my sleeping bag and rolled over with my back to the room and held Peter Wimsey so close to my eyes that I couldn't focus on the page.

So my friends thought I was so socially inept, so gullible, so desperate, that I had to be *protected* from Mackenzie Woodrow.

Sometimes the people who love you can hurt you most easily, even when they're trying to be kind.

Right at the start of camp, Bec and Iris and I had signed up for the Star Gazers Trek. Iris was crazy about astronomy, and of course she loved pondering the possibility of alien life forms and intergalactic travel and the vastness of the universe. She'd convinced Bec and me to come along with her; besides, I was mildly interested in the vastness of the universe too. She couldn't persuade Georgia, though. Georgia loved her sleep, and there was no way she was going to be dragged through the bush and forced to stay awake all night, peeing behind trees, lying on two millimetres of foam sleeping mat, so she could peer up at the sky.

The Star Gazers Trek involved a long afternoon hike up Mt Emmaline, then dinner over a campfire, and star maps after dark. We had to pack sleeping-bags and mats, but none of us expected to sleep much, out in the bush. Only a few girls had signed up, which added to the appeal.

Bec and I were rolling up our sleeping-bags after lunch when Iris appeared. 'Guess who's coming?'

'Georgia?'

'Nope.' Iris looked at Bec. 'Jem's new best friend, that's who. Mackenzie Woodrow.'

Mackenzie and I hadn't spoken since the Great Book Raid three days ago. Instantly I felt anxious. Now I'd have to watch what I said to her, conscious of Bec and Iris listening; or if I didn't talk to her, which was more likely, I'd be aware of her, observing a nerd in her natural habitat. Either way, it wouldn't be relaxing. Great. Mackenzie Woodrow had ruined the whole expedition and we hadn't even left yet.

The star-gazing party gathered by a corner of the dining shed. Mr Harmison – Glenn – was leading the trek. He was a science teacher. I'd never had much to do with him, but Iris said he was great. He was always laughing and cracking bad jokes. And he was really old, over forty – nearly as old as George Clooney.

'Only six of you? The elite! Seekers of celestial knowledge!'

He read our names off the roll. Bec, Iris, Mackenzie and me, Olivia Baxter and Emily Tan, also nerds, needless to say. Mackenzie Woodrow stuck out in this company like a lioness among a pack of alley cats. Or a shark in a school of goldfish. Even Glenn gave her a funny look. 'You do realise this trek is about astronomy, not astrology?' he said. 'Strictly no discussion of star signs or any of that nonsense.'

'I wouldn't dream of it,' said Mackenzie. 'I'm a Virgo. We're *very* sceptical about that kind of thing.'

Glenn barked a laugh; another instant member of the Mackenzie Woodrow Fan Club. 'Let's go.'

At first Bec and Iris and I walked together, but then the path narrowed – and got a lot steeper – and we slipped into single file. We soon ran out of breath for conversation.

I didn't have to worry about Mackenzie talking to me; she strode off in the lead with Glenn, chatting away and making him laugh, while the rest of us, the unsporty, unfit, nerdy ones, puffed and panted and struggled up the trail behind them. I didn't lift my eyes from my hiking boots (specially purchased for camp) for what seemed like hours, except when we paused to squeeze water down our throats and catch our breath.

The trail wound along Breakneck Ridge, and when we stopped, the slender gums stretched up all around us. A bellbird's call chimed through the bush; the clean scent of eucalyptus rose around us in the afternoon warmth. It was lovely. It would have been even lovelier if Olivia Baxter had shut up about her blisters.

Slowly, slowly, we trudged up that mountain. We'd been bushwalking, but nothing so steep, or so far. The shadows were long and the sun slanted orange through the trees when Glenn, who'd got a fair way ahead of the rest of us (with Mackenzie), yelled out, 'Coooo-eee! We're here!'

We emerged from the trees onto a plateau near the top of the mountain. The view was amazing. The whole plain was laid out at our feet: the brown winding ribbon of the river, teeny black dots of cows on yellow paddocks, the distant blue of the mountains gently receding to our left. We clutched our knees and gasped, 'Oh – wow,' and other lame exclamations of wonder.

'Looks like we'll have a clear night,' said Glenn. 'Not a cloud in the sky.'

He lit a fire and we cooked dehydrated stew out of foil packets for dinner. Mackenzie made jokes with Glenn about how it was impossible to tell what kind of animal we were eating.

'What a flirt,' muttered Iris.

I didn't say anything.

As we were wolfing down our chocolate bikkies for dessert, the sun set, and the darkness crept across the landscape below. First the sky was blue, then it went pale, almost white, and pink and yellow bands of colour glowed on the horizon; then slowly dark velvety blue washed through it, and suddenly it was night, and the flames of the campfire gave all our faces an orange glow. We toasted marshmallows, and Glenn made billy tea, which tasted rank.

Then Iris said, 'For Pete's sake, stop whinging about the tea, and just look at the sky!'

So we looked up. And right across the sky, so thick we could hardly see a space between them, were the stars. I'd never seen the stars like that in the city, so huge, and bright, and shining white. It was easy to believe they were distant suns. And there were so many. It was awesome — literally, awe-inspiring. If I were religious, it would have made me think about God; it made Iris think about the inevitability of aliens being out there *somewhere*.

Glenn let the fire die down. He passed round the tele-scope and told us where to look for Venus, and Sirius, and the double star of Antares, and the craters on the moon. Then he told us about nebulas, and dwarf stars, and black holes, and the Big Bang, and he and Iris had an argument about parallel universes. To be honest, I didn't care about the possibility of a parallel universe. All I wanted to do was to stare up at the stars.

Mackenzie's voice was quiet in my ear. 'Too much talk. Let's go.' She slipped into the shadows. I didn't even stop to think; I just followed her. It was pitch black, and away from the fire I couldn't see a thing. I tripped over a log and banged my ankle. 'Ow!'

Mackenzie giggled and out of the dark she grabbed my hand. 'Come on.'

We stumbled along the path in the blackness until the fire and the flickering shadows vanished and we couldn't hear the voices of the others. 'That's better,' said Mackenzie, and she pulled at my hand till I sat down.

'I swore a solemn oath never to hold hands with you,' I said.

'But *I* didn't swear never to hold hands with *you*.'

'Oh, well, that's all right then.'

We both lay back so we were staring straight up into the sky.

'I feel dizzy,' I said after a minute. 'I think I'm going to fall in.'

'Well, we would, if it wasn't for gravity,' said Mackenzie. 'Doesn't it make you feel small — we're just tiny ant-like creatures, clinging to a little planet, spinning in space. Just specks on a paltry pebble. And if there wasn't any gravity, we'd fly off into all that space . . .'

'Mackenzie?'

'Yes?'

'Shut up.'

She laughed, and shut up. And we lay there in the silence and the vastness of the universe, looking up — or down — at those slowly wheeling stars, still holding hands. And the weird thing is that it didn't feel strange. I didn't want to let go; the feeling of being about to fly off, to fall into space, was so strong, I needed some kind of anchor to the earth. Maybe Mackenzie felt the same, because she didn't let go either.

After a long time, Mackenzie whispered, 'You can almost hear them singing.'

'What would stars sing?' I whispered back.

'Radiohead,' said Mackenzie in the same dreamy voice, and we giggled.

Then I did something I never, never do, not in front of other people. Maybe because it was so dark, and I couldn't see her face, or because the magic of those stars was so strong, I began to sing. I sang a Radiohead song, and then I sang an old hymn we sing sometimes in assembly at school. I think I got some of the words wrong, but it sounded right somehow, singing in the dark, with all the stars flung out above our heads, in the middle of the bush.

And then I said:

'The stars fall,
silent as the snow,
and we fill our hands
with drifting blossom.'

Mackenzie was silent for a while, then she whispered, 'Is that a song?'

'No, I — I wrote it. I write poetry, sometimes.'

I'd never admitted that to anyone before. In the cool dark my face felt like fire.

'Jessica Martinic,' Mackenzie said softly. 'That was beautiful.'

And I knew she wasn't going to laugh at me. Slowly my face cooled, and then we lay watching the stars for a long, long time without saying anything. And happiness — no, it was a feeling of absolute joy — swelled up inside my chest like a balloon, and I could feel myself smiling in the dark, for no reason at all. For once, I wasn't worried about anything; I just knew everything was going to be fine. Better than fine: spectacular, marvellous, fabulous! The world was perfect and, at the same time, overflowing with possibility, and I felt I could hold it all in my cupped hands and drink — drink in the stars and fill up with light.

april

'Maybe we knew each other in a previous life,' said Mackenzie.

'Maybe we were sisters. Maybe twins.'

'Hm.' Mackenzie sounded doubtful. 'I can say whatever I want to you, and I know you'll understand exactly what I mean. That's never happened with *anyone*. Certainly not my sister . . .'

'It hasn't happened with me either.' I laughed into the phone.

'Are you thinking about Bec?'

'*Yes*. How did you know? She *never* gets what I'm talking about. That's amazing, how did you know I was thinking about her?'

'I noticed at camp. She seems to be the queen of the wilful misunderstanding.'

I laughed again. 'That's so true. I love her though.'

'Of course,' said Mackenzie.

I didn't feel qualified to analyse Mackenzie's friendships. Anyway, I didn't want to talk about Phillipa or Frances or Rosie Lee. I said, 'Do you think it's going to be hard?'

'When school starts?'

We were both quiet.

'I don't know,' said Mackenzie. 'What do you think?'

'We'll manage,' I said. How hard could it be? We'd spoken on the phone nearly every day of the holidays; Mackenzie had come round to my place twice in a week. Sure, we weren't 'out' as friends; we hadn't hung out in any of the places where Mackenzie's gang (or mine) would be likely to see us, but I had no desire to go to those places anyway. It was more fun to have Mackenzie come and take over our kitchen.

Already it was funny to think there was a time when I wasn't friends with Mackenzie. I sat up and shoved my feet into my thongs. 'I'd better go, dinner's nearly ready.'

'Wow, you eat early.'

'What time do you have dinner?'

'I dunno, eight, eight-thirty. Depends on Dad. I don't know why we bother though. He's hardly ever here for dinner no matter how long we wait.'

'He must work hard.'

'Yeah, he's trying to get into politics. Lots of meetings.' Mackenzie exaggerated a yawn.

'Oh. Right.' Politics was one subject I didn't want to discuss with Mackenzie; I had a feeling we might be on different sides, and I wasn't ready to tackle that just yet.

'Enemies forever,' she said, as if she'd read my mind.

'Enemies forever.'

'I'll call you tomorrow, let you know how yoga went.'

'Okay, bye.'

I hung up and wandered into the kitchen.

'Mackenzie again?' asked Mum.

'Mm.'

'It must be nice, having a new friend.'

'Mm.' It was true, I hadn't made any new friends – proper friends – since Bec and Iris and Georgia and I got together in Year 7. 'Do you want me to make the salad dressing?'

'Ooh, yes, thanks, darling.'

'Mackenzie says lemon juice is better than vinegar.'

'Does she? Okay, try that if you like.'

'What's that face for?'

Mum laughed. 'Sorry, I was just remembering . . . When I was your age I had such a crush on the girl across the street. She was *so* sophisticated. She was nineteen, her hair was so long she could sit on it, and she wore platform shoes. I wanted to *be* her. Deborah Wallace, her name was. I nearly called you Deborah, you know.'

'I haven't got a *crush* on Mackenzie Woodrow.'

'I didn't say you did.'

'Good.'

In fact I had been considering getting my hair cut — not exactly the same as hers, but slightly similar. But after Mum said that, I thought I'd better not. Not that Mackenzie would care, but other people might think I was copying her. Anyway, my hair's too curly.

The next morning, a letter arrived. A real letter, in a real envelope, in our real mailbox. Everyone's excited by a real letter, right? It's such a rarity. Even if it's only a card from Nana, there's still a frisson when I see my name on a real envelope. (Love that word, frisson. It's French, for *shiver*.)

I took it to my room. I didn't need to look at the bottom of the page to know who it was from.

To Jem

A season of stars
A green-eyed girl
The laughter of a river

The promise that things will be different now
Hope multiplying like stars,
Born in infinite emptiness,
Filling with light

Knowing you fills me with light
Ever expanding
Like the edge of the universe

One day, there will be only
Light

Yours, always
Mackenzie

I reread the poem a couple of times – okay, a couple of hundred times. Part of me was flattered, blown away; I nearly cried when I first read it, to tell the truth. I guessed I was supposed to be the green-eyed girl. And it was beautiful, *a season of stars* and everything.

But then . . . it was so extravagant, so emotional. *Knowing you fills me with light?* That was a huge thing to say to someone you didn't know very well.

Because in spite of what she said about feeling as if we'd known each other forever (and it's true, I felt like that too), I didn't actually know her well enough to be sure I could trust what she was saying. I kept hearing Bec and Iris in my head: *She's just using you.* Was Mackenzie messing with me? I was torn between feeling moved by what she'd written, wanting to believe it, and not wanting to get sucked in if she didn't mean it.

And then there was the way she'd signed off. What was that comma doing between *yours* and *always?* Was that a mistake, or did it mean something? And if it meant something, what exactly did it mean?

I was still brooding about it when Bec rang and invited me over. For about a tenth of a millisecond I considered showing her the poem. But of course I didn't.

Bec's brother Richard was there. I hadn't actually met him before. He was a couple of years older than us. This was the brother who'd just come back from India. He'd finished school really young, but his parents thought he wasn't ready for uni so they'd sent him overseas for a year. We sat around chatting for a while, about India. He said it was full on, the smells, the noise, the poverty, but really beautiful too.

'You were brave to go on your own,' I said, and he and Bec yelped with laughter.

'On my own! I wish! I had an uncle or an aunty or a cousin fifteen times removed with me every second!'

'Oh, right, of course.' I felt like a complete idiot.

'I'm sick of hearing about India,' announced Bec. 'Let's go to a movie.'

'*Flying the Kite*'s supposed to be good,' I volunteered.

'Okay, whatever, I just want to go out. The best thing about having a brother old enough to drive is that he can take us places. Come on, Richard.'

'She's much nicer to me since I got my licence, in fact.' Richard grinned at me.

I expected Richard to drop us off at the cinema, but he came to the movie, too. I didn't tell Bec, of course, but I'd picked the film because Mackenzie had raved about it, and I loved it, though at times I did have trouble concentrating. Phrases from Mackenzie's poem echoed in my head. How should I respond? Mackenzie had said she was going to ring tonight. I couldn't ignore it. What should I say? Should I write her a poem back? *God*, I couldn't do that . . .

'Hello? Earth to Jem, are you receiving?' Bec waved a hand in front of my face. The credits were over. 'Do you want a juice or something? Or do you have to go straight home?'

Richard bought pancakes and hot chocolates and we talked about his course at uni, and his new part-time job with an aid agency. 'It doesn't pay much, in fact, but I think I'll learn a lot.' He had to maintain their website and put together their e-newsletter. It sounded interesting, but I was a bit distracted.

After the pancakes Richard drove me home. He parked in our driveway and I scooted out of the back seat. Richard wound down his window. 'We should do this again, yeah? Plenty of holidays left before you guys go back, aren't there? What if I pick you up on Tuesday afternoon?'

'Yeah, okay, that'd be good.' I waved. 'See ya, Bec.'

'See ya!' she yelled from the front seat.

Mackenzie rang at seven-thirty on the dot. I wondered as I answered the phone if she'd organised to ring and tell me about yoga as an excuse; she knew I'd get the poem today.

'I got the poem,' I said immediately.

'Did you?' For the first time ever, Mackenzie sounded shy.

'It's beautiful.'

'Really?'

We both fell silent; I couldn't think what else to say.

'So how was yoga?'

'Oh, you know. Serene.'

We both laughed, and everything was okay.

'I thought of the perfect job for you,' said Mackenzie.

'What?'

'Editor,' said Mackenzie triumphantly. 'What do you think?'

'Ye-eah? What does an editor do?'

'*Reads*, of course. And corrects people's mistakes.'

'Perfect.'

'It is perfect. It uses all your strengths. Don't you think?'

'Mm, maybe.'

'You should try and get on the magazine committee next year, for practice.'

'Let me think about it.'

'Am I being bossy? I am, aren't I.'

'No, you're not. If you were, I'd say.'

'Would you? Jem, will you promise me always to tell me if I do something to upset you? Don't let it . . . fester.'

'Yeah, I'll tell you, I promise.' And I laughed: as if Mackenzie could ever upset me. Ye gods, as Peter Wimsey would say.

On Tuesday, Richard came to pick me up just after lunch. I heard him chatting to Mum while I was in the bathroom, and when I came out she said, 'He's waiting in the car.'

'Okay.' I kissed her goodbye.

'Jem? Here's twenty dollars. Just in case.'

'Thanks — I should have enough, though.'

'Just in case,' she repeated, and I thought she gave me a strange look, but I didn't realise why until I got in the car.

'Hi, Jem.'

'Hi . . . Where's Bec?'

'Bec wasn't invited.'

'Oh!' It took me a minute to process this. 'But — I thought we were all—'

Richard took his hand off the ignition. 'It's not too late to change your mind.'

'No,' I said after a second. 'I mean, I'm not changing it. I just didn't realise . . .' I felt weird even saying it, in case I still hadn't understood. Had he really asked me on — a *date*? My first date, and I was too socially inept to realise I'd been asked?

'Good,' said Richard, and started the car.

If I'd known it was a *date*, I would have been nervous for days beforehand. I would have agonised about what to wear, if my hair was okay, if I should wear make-up. But because I thought I was just going to the movies with Bec, I wasn't wearing anything special, I hadn't even combed my hair before I'd left. No wonder Mum was giving me funny looks. At least I'd brushed my teeth. For Pete's sake. What if Richard tried to *kiss* me? I didn't know how to behave, what to say, where to look.

Trust me, I was hardly what Lord Peter might call a picturesque young lady. I had stumpy legs, no waist, I could never find clothes that flattered my figure, I didn't even know where to start. I hated shopping. No matter how my thick hair was cut, it never held a shape. And my face — well, if I scrutinised each feature individually, they seemed okay. There were no elements missing; it was the way they fitted together that was unsatisfactory. My face was quite broad. *Slavic cheekbones*, Dad said. But I thought I looked more like an Eskimo. When I smiled, my eyes disappeared.

When Bec had been with us last week I hadn't given a moment's thought to my appearance. It had never crossed my mind that Richard was looking at me, that he might consider me that way, as a possible date. A possible *girlfriend*?

I sat stiffly in the front seat, mumbling stilted replies to Richard's questions about what I'd been up to in the last few days (basically nothing), while my mind churned around like a whirlpool. Why hadn't Bec warned me? Was my hair sticking out at the side? Why had I worn those terrible jeans that made my bum look huge? Because they were comfortable, which was ironic — I'd never felt less comfortable in my life.

As I trudged alongside him through the shopping centre I thought, *at least I won't have to suffer through this again*, because there was no way he would ever ask me twice. And as soon as I thought that, I relaxed and it got easier.

Actually I rather liked the feeling of walking with a boy at my side. Richard wasn't stunningly good-looking, and he was kind of short, not that I care, being so short myself, and his features didn't fit together effortlessly either . . . but, you know, he was eighteen, and he was with me. And that made me feel good. Me! The Invisible Girl, nerdy Jem, on a date!

We watched a film — he liked it, I didn't — and we had a good argument about it over pancakes, which was better than sitting in silence, and I even found myself thinking I was having a good time.

But on the way home I was paralysed with nerves. Would he ask me out again? Did I *want* to go out again? He wouldn't ask me. No, it was over. It was pleasant enough, and it was over. I'd survived my first date, phew. No need to feel heartbroken, Richard was no Peter Wimsey. It was good practice, that was all . . .

'So,' said Richard.

'So,' I said. I already had my hand on the door. 'Thanks. That was fun.'

'No, no, thank *you*.'

'Um . . .' I didn't have to ask him in, did I? Not with Mum at home! And people only did that in American sitcoms, didn't they? He hadn't turned off the engine. If he wanted to come in, he'd have turned off the engine, wouldn't he? I said, 'Say hi to Bec for me.'

'I will.' He had this kind of expectant expression and I had *no idea* what he was waiting for.

'Okay then,' I said finally. 'See you,' and I opened the car door.

Then he leaned over and said, 'May I call you again, Jem?'

Now that was straight out of an American sitcom. I had to stop myself from laughing. I managed to say, 'Okay.' Then I banged the door shut and ran inside and it was such a *relief* to be safe in the house and out of that car and away from that terrible awkwardness.

I took the phone into my room.

'Guess what I did today.'

'Went to the movies with Bec.'

'Close. With Bec's brother. No Bec.'

'No Bec? Bec didn't come? Why not?'

'Well, she was never coming. Apparently. I just didn't realise.'

There was a brief pause, then Mackenzie shrieked. 'He asked you *out* and you didn't realise? Jem. *The universe throws us gifts.* So? Did you have a good time? Do you like him?'

'He didn't ask me out. We went to a movie.'

'What do you think asking out *is*? Of course he asked you out. And you haven't answered my question. Do you like him?'

I chewed on my thumbnail while I considered Richard as boyfriend material. Mackenzie was very quiet. 'I dunno,' I said at last. 'I don't *dislike* him.'

'But is he hot? Do you want him?'

That's not a question Bec or Iris would have asked, about any boy, in a million years. I didn't know if it was even a question I would have asked myself. Mackenzie put it so bluntly. We were so different, our worlds were so different. Mackenzie had probably had sex. I'd never been remotely near it – no, hang on, a boy had asked me out. I was getting nearer by the minute.

I said, 'He asked if he could call me.'

Mackenzie let out a long breath. 'So he wants you.'

'*No-o-o*! No, no, no.'

'Obviously he does. Trust me, *I* know *all* about boys.'

She sounded strange; I guessed she'd begun to comprehend, too, how different we were, how naive I was, what a child. I wished I hadn't told her.

Mackenzie said briskly, 'So the big question is, do you want him?'

'I don't know,' I said. 'No – not yet, anyway.'

'Good answer,' said Mackenzie. 'Sometimes it takes a while to realise that you're attracted to someone. Then all of a sudden, when you least expect it, bam, it hits you. Like a truck. And nothing's ever the same again.'

'Because you've been squashed into a two-dimensional object.' I was trying to make her laugh; she sounded – weary, jaded, as if she'd had her heart broken a million times. Maybe she had. I was too shy to ask. I couldn't imagine it, though; much more likely that she'd broken a million hearts.

She did laugh, and I felt better. She said, 'Promise me one thing, Jem. Don't rush into anything — anything physical, will you.'

'I don't think there's much chance of that. Believe me, this was not the world's most passionate date. I don't think he'll ring. He was just being polite. He's very polite.'

'Really?' Mackenzie sounded brighter. 'Well, you never know. I bet he does ring. Wait and see.'

And then of course he didn't.

For a few days my heart seized up when I heard the phone, but it was never Richard. I couldn't ring Bec, in case he answered (Bec's parents refused to buy her a mobile till she turned sixteen). But after a while I stopped expecting him to call. I knew he was just being polite. I knew he wouldn't ring. So I could hardly be disappointed.

But it was still . . . humiliating.

'Well,' said Mackenzie. 'You didn't want him anyway. It'd be much worse if he did want you, and he was hanging around with puppy dog eyes and you couldn't get rid of him and you just wanted to kick him in the teeth.'

'This is something that's happened to you?' I had to laugh, she sounded so vicious.

'Oh, God, yeah.' Poor Mackenzie, tormented by all her rejected boyfriends. It was lucky Bec and Iris couldn't hear her.

'Mackenzie?'

'Mm?'

'Are you – are you going out with anyone now?'

'Are you kidding? You think if I was going out with anyone I'd have time to crap on to you on the phone every night? No way. No, I'm not going out with anyone. Anyway, as if I wouldn't have told you!'

'Mm.' Of course she would have told me. If you really like someone, you can't keep it a secret.

'School tomorrow.'

'Can't wait,' drawled Mackenzie. She yawned. 'Better get our beauty sleep. Enemies forever.'

'Enemies forever. Bye.'

april

'Hey, Martinic.'

'Hey!'

I'd been nervous about seeing Mackenzie again — not throwing-up nervous, just butterflies. I kept jumping, and laughing too loudly, and trying to be casual and relaxed, in case she came up behind me while I wasn't looking. Then she came up behind me when I wasn't looking.

I'd forgotten how golden she was.

'Isn't it weird to be back,' she said.

'Everything looks the wrong size. Too big. Or too small. Like everything's grown while we were away.' What was wrong with me? I was prattling like a fool.

But Mackenzie smiled. 'Or shrunk.'

'It's like when the aliens kidnap someone and replace

them with an identical replica. Everything in the school's been replaced with identical replicas.'

'But the replicas can't be exactly identical or we wouldn't realise they were replicas.'

'No, the aliens must get it slightly wrong . . .'

This was the sort of discussion that Iris and I could keep up for hours. Why was I having a conversation from deep, deep nerdworld with Mackenzie Woodrow? Because suddenly she was Mackenzie Woodrow again, and I'd forgotten how to talk to her. I was an identical replica of myself, and so was she.

As if she'd read my mind, Mackenzie leaned forward, so her golden hair swung against her cheekbone, and whispered, 'I hope the real Jem and the real Mackenzie are having a good time, wherever they are.'

'Probably on a spaceship somewhere. Drinking space cocktails.'

'Spocktails.'

'Hey, you've been brushing up on your nerd phrase book. I'm impressed.'

Mackenzie grinned, and for a second she wasn't perfectly groomed, poised, polished Mackenzie Woodrow; she was just another idiot like me. We smiled at each other behind the screen of the open locker door, our faces close together. Then she pulled away.

'Gotta go.'

And she glided away down the corridor to where

Rosie Lee and Phillipa and her hangers-on were waiting.

I'd nurtured a tiny hope that Mackenzie and I might be in the same form for term two. We weren't. But Bec and Iris and Georgia and I were, for the first time ever: Lab 5, our new home. The Year 10s were in the science wing, because we were mature enough not to turn on all the taps and flood the place.

Not that we were acting mature that morning. Everyone was squealing and running amok (that's a Malay word – for *acting like idiots*, presumably). The whole of Year 10 had forgotten how to act at school. We were accustomed to the freedoms of Heathersett River – wearing shorts and tracksuits (albeit navy blue school shorts and tracksuits), being outdoors all the time, never sitting at a desk. All of which meant we were pretty rowdy for the first week or so; for the first day of term we were practically uncontrollable.

Bec didn't say anything about Richard, and I was far too embarrassed to mention him. It seemed that we were going to let the subject fade away, and that was fine with me.

The whole school gathered in the Hall for morning assembly. Usually we sang a hymn (because it was a church school), and someone gave a presentation, and then notices were announced, and the Head led a prayer, and we all filed out again.

Trish — we had to call her Ms Wells again now, of course — took assembly. She spoke about Heathersett River, about how the whole of Year 10 had experienced a very special moment of togetherness and harmony, and how she fervently hoped that we would carry that through the rest of the year, and indeed the rest of our time at school, and who knows, maybe even the rest of our lives. 'It was one of the most inspirational moments of my career,' she said, and she touched the corner of her eye with her fingertip to signify strong emotion.

There was a considerable amount of mortified foot-shuffling and murmuring from Year 10, and everyone was relieved when she finished and the Head rose majestically and started going through the notices.

Mackenzie stopped me in the quad after assembly.

'So?'

'So what?'

'Are you going to try out?'

'For what?'

'Weren't you listening? Miss Macmillan needs people to read poems for the concert in term three. You should audition. You can speak poetry. You're a poet, for Pete's sake.'

'No *way*! I'd rather die.'

'But you'd be amazing.' Mackenzie gave me a meaningful look.

I glanced around and lowered my voice. 'You wouldn't tell anyone . . . about that night?'

'Of course not, never.' Mackenzie touched my sleeve and her eyes took on a mischievous gleam. 'I might just put your name down anyway.'

'*No!* You can't— I can't *perform.* Mackenzie, I'd never forgive you.'

'Okay, I'm kidding.' She shook her head. 'It's just *reading.* It's nothing.'

I pulled a complicated face, intended to convey admiration for Mackenzie's own gifts, and simultaneous shock and amazement at the very thought that she might entertain a glimmer of an idea that I might share even a fraction of those same gifts, and that I was running late and had to go.

I think she got it. She was pretty good at reading my mind.

But it haunted me, that conversation. It reminded me how precious that night on the mountain was, and how fragile; how easily she could expose it to other people, and ruin it; how easily she could hurt me, if she wanted to.

Anyway, she didn't put my name down. She didn't put her name down either. But Miss Macmillan had a quiet word and more or less ordered her to audition. And when the final list of performers was announced a couple of weeks later, naturally Mackenzie Woodrow's name was at the top.

A week later Bec and Iris and Georgia were standing in a huddle in front of the Lab 5 lockers.

'Where have you been?' asked Bec crossly.

'Nowhere.' Mackenzie had abducted me to go to the bookroom with her. 'What's going on?'

'Nothing,' said Georgia.

'Georgia's going to a party,' said Iris, in a tone that suggested Georgia had proposed to amputate a limb.

'Whose party?'

'I don't know exactly.' Georgia looked nervous.

'So why are you going?'

'Rosie asked me to.'

'You can't go to a party with Rosie Lee!' Bec put her hands on her hips and thrust her sharp little nose at Georgia. 'You don't know what might happen!'

'Rosie asked me to go with her – to look after her.'

'She's got her own friends!' said Bec. 'Why does she have to drag you into it?'

'Rosie needs all the friends she can get. You don't know what it's like for her, what she has to put up with at home . . .'

'Oh, Rosie Lee and her tortured home life!' snorted Iris. 'Tell her, Jem. She can't go. I've heard about these parties.' She folded her arms. 'Does your mum know, Georgia?'

I banged my locker shut and turned the key. 'Why shouldn't Georgia go to a party if her mum says it's okay?'

'Thanks, Jem,' muttered Georgia, but she didn't look

particularly grateful. She looked as if she were about to cry. Maybe her mum didn't think it was okay.

'Friends watch out for each other,' said Bec loudly. 'Iris and I care about Georgia, even if *you* don't think it's important.'

I said, 'Well, isn't that—'

'What?'

'Isn't that the point? Georgia's being a friend to Rosie, she's going to look out for her.'

'Great. And when she gets her drink spiked, and gets raped, and knifed in the gutter, and beaten up.'

'Oh, for Pete's sake, Iris. All at one party?'

'You think you're so smart, Jem, but you've never been to one of these parties. Why don't you get your friend Mackenzie Woodrow to tell you what goes on?'

'I will. I'm sure it's not this — this hysterical orgy of drugs and sex and violence . . .' A thought struck me. 'I know, why don't we all go? Then we can all watch out for Georgia.'

Silence. Bec and Iris shuffled their feet.

'But we're not invited,' said Iris.

'It's my dad's birthday dinner that night, actually,' said Bec.

I said, 'And there's that English assignment . . .'

'Where *is* Georgia?' said Bec suddenly.

We glared at each other. Little Sonia Darcy pointed down the hallway. 'She ran into the toilets.'

We swooped in after her, but Georgia wanted Bec, even though I was the one who'd stuck up for her. That's gratitude for you. Then the bell rang and Iris dragged me away; she was paranoid about being late.

I *would* talk to Mackenzie, I decided as I ran. She'd know the drill; she could tell me if we should be worried about Georgia, if these parties were okay, if Rosie Lee was going to get Georgia into trouble. Maybe Georgia just wanted a reason to refuse without upsetting Rosie. Obviously Mackenzie had a good reason, or she'd be going to the party with Rosie herself . . .

I slipped into the chair beside Iris feeling better now I had a plan. In terms of — I don't know, worldly knowledge? sophistication? — Mackenzie was as far ahead of me as I was ahead of Bec. Bec had no clue, I had some clue, and Mackenzie had heaps of clue. She was the grand master of clue. She was the Clue Queen. She had more clues than Lord Peter Wimsey.

'Jem? Are you with us in mind as well as in body?' Mrs Hewlett's beady eye was on me, and I hastily flipped to the right page and summoned my best intellectual frown, to show I was deep in profound thought and constructing a detailed historical analysis of the text.

It was good to have a reason to call Mackenzie. She called me most nights before I could think up an excuse for calling her; I felt I should have some pretext, however lame it was. But it didn't seem to bother her; she didn't need a reason. She was more confident than me; she never had to wonder if the person she was calling actually wanted to hear from her . . .

'*Jessica Martinic*! I asked you a question.'

Gulp. Iris came to my rescue, whispering, 'Causes of the French Revolution,' and I reeled off the answer. Iris frowned at me. At this rate I was going to lose all my nerd credentials: running late, not paying attention in class. Next thing you know, I might get something *wrong*, and it would be all over. I'd be expelled from nerd-dom, thrown into the wilderness. Then what would become of me? I shivered, and stared at my textbook, and this time I really did try to concentrate.

That night at home, I was unpacking my bag when I found a small parcel wrapped in purple tissue paper. It was heavy, and it clinked. When I unwrapped it, a necklace fell out of the paper onto my bed – three strands of green glass beads.

A present. I upended my bag, but there was no card, no note, nothing; an anonymous present. I tried it on. It was gorgeous, just perfect for my colouring. It even made me look – sort of casually glamorous.

Dad yelled, 'It's that Mackenzie girl on the phone!'

She was early. I hurried to the phone and took it back to my room. 'I just found the weirdest thing in my bag!'

'Really? What?'

'A necklace. Green beads, it's beautiful. Do you think . . .' I hesitated to even suggest it. 'Do you think Richard might have asked Bec to put it in my bag? There's no note or anything, but it must be him, mustn't it?'

'Why must it be him?'

'Well, it's jewellery. Isn't that the kind of thing a boy gives a girl? And he's the only boy I know.'

There was a brief pause, then Mackenzie laughed. 'Can't you think of another scenario?'

'Oh. You think it's a mistake? Maybe it's really Bec's? We share a locker, it might have fallen into my bag by mistake – but she didn't—'

'No, you idiot,' interrupted Mackenzie. 'It's for you. But it's not from Bec's brother. It's from me.'

'From you? Oh – wow – Mackenzie.'

'You didn't text him thank you or anything excruciating like that, did you?'

'No, no, of course not. But Mackenzie – they're gorgeous. You shouldn't have.'

'They weren't expensive. And even if they were, I'm loaded, remember?'

'That's not what I meant—' I stopped. What did I mean? I said, 'They're just – too beautiful.'

'It's nothing, Jem. I saw them, and they were pretty, and I knew they'd suit you. That's all. It's just a present, no big deal.'

'They do suit me.'

'Yes. They reminded me of your eyes.'

There was a strange silence. At last I said, 'Well . . . thanks. Thank you.'

'So you like them?'

'I do. I love them.'

'Do you? Really? You love them?'

'Yes, of course I do.'

Then there was another strange silence.

'Well,' I said at last. 'I'd better go. See you tomorrow.'

'See you tomorrow.'

I held the beads between my fingers for a long time. I tried them on again and stared at myself in the mirror. Then I took them off. I could have hung them on the side of the mirror with the silver chain Nana gave me – the one I never wear – and the imitation pearls I keep in honour of Harriet Vane. But instead I hid them under my bed, in the box where I kept Mackenzie's poem. I don't know why. I guess I didn't want Mum to ask about them. It was like the poem, in a way – they were too much. Beautiful, amazing, wonderful. But too much.

A bit like Mackenzie herself. Too good to be true. Too rich for ordinary consumption. I don't mean loaded rich, I mean rich as in food. (I consulted the dictionary and there wasn't a good definition; it just said, *with a high proportion of butter, oil, eggs, spices etc.*, which is a really clumsy, inelegant definition, in my humble opinion, and it doesn't convey the meaning either, which is basically: this is delicious, but too much of it will make you sick.)

The next morning I realised I'd forgotten to ask Mackenzie about Georgia and Rosie Lee and the whole party situation. Well, it didn't matter. I could talk to her about it later. There was plenty of time.

But that was the day it all fell apart.

There was no sign, no warning. Unless the beads were an omen I was too dense to interpret; an omen that meant the exact opposite of what it seemed to mean.

After assembly I got caught in a clot of people by the quadrangle doors, just behind Mackenzie.

'Hello, Mackenzie.'

She didn't hear me.

'Hey, Woodrow!' I said, slightly louder.

Very, very slowly, she swung around. She was about a head taller than I was, but at that moment she seemed to tower over me. She looked at me for a second or two, then she said, in a cool, distant voice, 'Oh, hi, Jessica.'

Not Jem, not Martinic: Jessica. As if we'd never even met.

I was shell-shocked, and she swept away. Between Phillipa and Frances, laughing.

Rosie Lee lingered, smirking over her shoulder. 'Is she bored with you now?' she murmured. 'Poor little Jem . . .' Then she vanished too.

'Jem! Hurry along please. You've been told often enough not to clog up the doorways.'

'Sorry, Mrs Peterson.'

I moved, but I was in a daze; I didn't know where I was walking. I felt ridiculous, and tears prickled in my eyes, as if I were a baby.

'Did you hear Rosie sniggering?' Iris said indignantly, and immediately I felt better. Slightly better.

Georgia grabbed my arm and squeezed it. 'Rosie wasn't laughing at *you*,' she said. 'She was laughing at Mrs Peterson.'

I knew that wasn't true, but it was irrelevant. Rosie could have stripped off naked and waggled her bare bum at me for all I cared. I didn't give a damn about Rosie Lee.

'They're both cows,' said Bec cheerfully, appearing behind us.

'*Vipers*,' said Iris with relish.

Nobody said, *we warned you, Jem*, but they didn't have to.

Part of me was in denial. I half-expected Mackenzie to rush up to me outside the lockers or in the toilets and say, 'Hey, Martinic, you didn't think I meant it, did you?' But she didn't.

Okay, I thought. Something's happened. Something that was preventing her from talking to me, temporarily. I couldn't for the life of me imagine what that something might be, but I clung to the possibility all day, and the day after, and the day after that. Maybe terrorists were holding her family hostage. Maybe she had a disease of the vocal cords and couldn't speak. Maybe she had amnesia. Maybe aliens had possessed her and she was protecting me by pretending she didn't know me. Maybe she'd been kidnapped and this was the identical replica of Mackenzie who wasn't quite right.

Maybe she just didn't like me any more.

Maybe she thought I'd been sucking up to her, trying to get into the cool gang. But she *knew* I didn't care about that . . .

Maybe I hadn't been enthusiastic enough about the necklace. Maybe I'd been too enthusiastic.

Maybe she thought I had a crush on her.

Bec and Iris and Georgia were extra cheerful for the rest of the week. I couldn't decide if it was because a) they'd been proven right about Mackenzie being superficial; b) they knew I was miserable and they were trying to cheer me up; or c) I wasn't friends with Mackenzie any more, so now I'd have more time to hang out with them. It was true, I had neglected them a tiny bit. Not that I'd ever actually *dropped* them. Not like Mackenzie had just dropped me.

The weekend came. I guess I'd hoped in the back of my mind that whatever had caused this abrupt cold-shouldering might be school-related, and maybe at the weekend she might tell me what was going on. Or she'd ring as usual and everything would be fine again.

But as the weekend wore on with no signal from her, a cold knot of hurt began to replace the fog of bewilderment I'd been bumping around in all week. Even if she *did* ring, I wouldn't know what to say to her. Was I supposed to apologise? What had I done wrong? Even if *she* apologised, what explanation would be good enough? What could possibly make this all right?

On Sunday night I lay sleepless in bed. It all meant nothing. The night we drank in the stars. Swimming in the river, hiking, the Great Book Raid. The phone calls, all the conversations. The poem. The necklace. It was all a joke, or a misunderstanding. I'd been stupid, gullible, naive − I didn't know *what* I'd been. Was I too ugly, too nerdy? Had I said something, done something, *not* done something, offended her somehow? It must have been my fault.

Or maybe the girls were right, and she was just a shallow, using viper-cow. But even as I was hating her, wishing I'd never met her, I couldn't quite believe that. The Mackenzie I knew wasn't like that; not my Mackenzie.

So why − and I know this is what Mum would have said if I'd told her about it, which is why I didn't − why I didn't ring her and say, '*For Pete's sake!* I thought we were friends. What's the story?'

I probably should have. But I couldn't pick up the phone. Whatever her reason was, I didn't want to hear it, I didn't want it confirmed. If I knew nothing, there was the hope (a tiny, ever-diminishing hope) that *today* Mackenzie would see me in the corridor and smile. That tonight the phone would ring, and she'd say, *I'm so, so sorry*.

A few times in the weeks that followed, I took out Mackenzie's poem from under the bed and read it again, in case the words had altered, in case there was an ironic interpretation that I'd been too dense to see. I held the glass beads and touched them with my fingertips. But I didn't put them on.

Then I stopped taking them out of the box. I left them under the bed, in the dark.

may

Halfway through term two, when I had completely and utterly forgotten that he even existed, Richard Patel called.

He rang on a Saturday morning when I was still lounging around in my jamies and said he'd pick me up in an hour. An hour! I was so dumbfounded I could hardly speak. 'Er . . . um . . . okay,' I said.

'Don't you want to know where we're going?'

'Um . . . yeah.'

'I thought we might go to that exhibition in the city, the botanical drawings, in fact? Because you said you were interested in plants.'

I had no memory of saying such a thing. But then I didn't have a clear memory of any of my conversations with Richard. I'd glazed over a few times and nodded and smiled. I guess I'd nodded and smiled at the wrong moment, and now he'd got the misconception that I had a passionate interest in botanical drawings. But it was too late to clear that up.

'Is Bec coming?' I blurted, just before he hung up.

There was a funny little silence, and then he said slowly, 'No-o. Would you like her to?'

'Well,' I said feebly. 'If she's interested . . .'

'I think she's busy, in fact.'

'Oh, okay. Never mind.'

'See you in an hour then?'

I stood for a minute with the phone in my hand. Why had I said that? Did I want Bec to come? To protect me? Would Richard think I didn't like him? *Did* I like him? He'd think I was an idiot. Did I care if he thought I was an idiot? Yes, I did. Did that mean I liked him? 'I just don't know,' I said aloud.

'Talking to yourself,' said Dad, walking past. 'First sign of madness.'

Dad could be very irritating sometimes.

So I went on my second date.

I was better prepared this time. While I was in the shower, I thought of things to talk about. But as it turned out, Richard didn't need any help. He apologised for not calling for so long; he'd been busy with uni and the new job. He told me about his new job. For hours. He described every single person he was working with, every task he'd performed. He practically drew me a map of the building. By the time we got to the city and had brunch at a little laneway cafe and found the exhibition at the library, I was longing for him to shut up.

I thought the exhibition would be boring, but it wasn't. The drawings were so detailed, so loving. It reminded me of Heathersett River, and being out in the bush, how beautiful it was, the birds and the trees and the sound of the river, and suddenly I missed it so much. I missed being happy.

When we emerged, the city seemed dirty and noisy. I wanted to get off the streets, but I didn't know where else to go.

Richard said, 'Would you like a drink?'

'What, in a bar?'

'No, of course not, you're underage, in fact.' He looked horrified. I was a tiny bit disappointed — I'd never been to a bar. It might have been a thrill, to go into a bar and have an illegal drink with a boy, on a date. Even in broad daylight.

I said, 'It'd be nice to go somewhere quiet.'

'Why don't we walk through the gardens?' he suggested.

'*Yes*, that'd be perfect!'

He smiled.

The gardens were green and still, and full of trees starting to shed their leaves, and the traffic was barely a murmur in the background. We walked past a dried-up fountain, and the famous Fairy Tree, and a statue of a long-dead, forgotten governor. It was sunny, not at all cold. Then we sat under a big spreading oak tree, and picked at the grass and talked. At least Richard talked; he told me more about India, and how his relatives thought he'd gone there to find a bride, which is hilarious, because he's only eighteen.

And then, without any warning, he leaned over and pushed his mouth at me. Our lips smashed together and his tongue shoved against my teeth. It was like that old TV ad where the tongue crawls out of its owner's mouth in search of beer. It wriggled and humped around like a miniature skinned ferret. Well, that skinned ferret was thrusting itself inside my mouth.

I pulled away and gasped, 'No, no!' and we fell away from each other and sat there on the grass breathing hard and not looking at each other.

I was so upset I almost cried. My first kiss, and it was *horrible*. I'd never have a first kiss again, and that was it, ruined.

Of course I'd imagined it a million times, often with Lord Peter Wimsey, played by a hot actor, but always there'd been a *conversation* beforehand. The conversation was almost more important than the kiss itself — there'd been meaningful looks, then he'd take my hand and meet my eyes, and say . . . something sensitive or witty or suddenly serious, and my heart would beat faster, and slowly his face would draw nearer, and our lips would meet softly, and part, and it would be exquisite, and shivery and slow, and gentle – it might become heated and passionate later on, but it would be a gradual build-up, a gradual *mutual* build-up . . .

But not *this*. This was like having a train crash into my face. I didn't expect a tongue to be *hard*, and rude, poking in like that, mashing my lips against my teeth. It was more like being punched than being kissed. And it was *embarrassing*. There were people walking by. I never thought my first kiss would be a public spectacle.

And . . . I'd thought my first kiss would be with a boy I'd be longing to kiss, a boy I was in love with. I was still trying to decide if I liked Richard. Though 'in fact' this had pretty much made up my mind.

Richard said in a stiff voice, 'Would you like to go home?'

I stood at once. 'Yes, please.'

We didn't say a word on the long walk back to the car. It was hideous. I knew I had to say something, to try to return things to normal, to erase that scene in the park. As Richard drove, I *forced* myself to speak.

'How many people work in the Melbourne office?'

'I told you, about twenty.' His voice was still stiff, more offended now, if anything, because I hadn't been listening.

'And – in Sydney?'

'About forty. I told you that, too.'

Our words fell into the heavy silence like lead pellets. Richard slammed on the brakes at the third red light in a row and swore under his breath. I was flung against the seatbelt, but Richard didn't even glance at me, let alone apologise. I clenched my hands in my lap, counting the minutes till I'd be safe at home. I just wanted to get as far away from Richard Patel as possible.

At first I'd felt like crying, but now I was angry. He'd kissed me – he didn't bother finding out if I wanted to kiss him – he'd just jumped on me and rammed his tongue down my throat! And *he* was all huffy with *me*? Maybe I should have just kissed him, and pretended to like it, that might have been easier . . .

But no, it wouldn't, because then he might have wanted to kiss me again, and then maybe more, and then I would have missed my chance to say, *No! Stop! I don't want to*. It just got worse and worse . . .

Richard stopped the car in front of my house. 'Well,' he said. 'Thank you for a nice day.'

'Yes. Thanks.'

We glared at each other. No nonsense about *I'll ring you* this time. I got out of the car and sprinted inside.

Mum said, 'How was—?'

I sped straight past her and into my room and slammed the door and threw myself on my bed. I pressed my face into the pillow as if I could scour the memory of that kiss away. It was all so *absurd*. Why did it have to be awkward and fumbling and embarrassing? Why couldn't it be the way it is in books and movies?

After a while Mum knocked, and I made room for her on the end of the bed. 'Not so good?' she said.

'Not so good.'

'Are you all right? Do you want to talk about it?'

'No,' I said. 'But I can tell you Richard Patel and I are never going to see each other again. Mum?' I felt silly asking, but I did anyway. 'Mum, could you read to me?'

Mum laughed, but she looked almost as if *she* were going to cry. She used to read to me every night, right up till high school, when I made her stop. But I can't tell you how comforting it was, curled up on my bed next to Mum while she read me Harry Potter. It was like Milo for the soul. I felt like a little kid.

What I really wished I could ask her was, am I normal? Was it normal to want to scrub my mouth out, and wash away the feeling of that *tongue* probing between my teeth? Was there something wrong with me? I wondered, if the tongue in question had belonged to Peter Wimsey, would I have found the sensation so repellent? It was hard to say. But I couldn't arrange to have my first kiss from a fictional character, could I. Especially not now.

Bec sprang at me first thing on Monday morning. I was anxious about seeing her. I wasn't sure what Richard might have said, but apparently he hadn't said anything – nothing bad, anyway.

'So how'd it go?' she said.

'Yeah. Good. The exhibition was . . . really interesting.'

'You had a good time, then?'

'Um, yeah.'

'Richard's cool, don't you think?'

'Um, yeah. He's got an interesting job. He's – nice.'

Bec smiled, and I realised I was probably giving her the wrong idea about how successful our date was. 'Bec?'

'Yes?'

What could I say without being rude? Bec was one of my best friends, and the last thing I wanted to do was upset her. I said, 'Nothing.' I stacked my books in my locker and slammed the door. Hopefully that would be the end of that. It wasn't as if Richard was ever going to call me again.

Ker-ching! Wrong again.

He called on Tuesday. We were just about to leave the house to go to Mum's friend Anna's for dinner when the phone rang; the answering machine picked it up.

'Jem, this is Richard Patel? I was calling to . . . see if we could do something this weekend? I could show you where I work, in fact, if you're interested? All right, thank you, bye.'

Mum and I stared at each other, frozen in the doorway. Dad growled, 'Who's this? Who's this person?'

'*Dad*. It's Bec's brother. I *told* you.'

Mum said, 'I thought you were never going to see each other again.'

'I thought so, too,' I groaned. '*Why*, why would he call me?'

But I knew why. That stupid conversation with Bec. She must have told him I liked him, that I had a wonderful time, that I couldn't wait to be his girlfriend. She'd taken my lukewarm remarks and heated them up to rampant enthusiasm.

'Call him back,' said Mum. 'Break it off quickly. You have to be firm.'

'I can't call him back now, we're going to Anna's.'

'*Who* is this person?' said Dad again. 'Jem, is this your boyfriend?'

'*No!*'

'But, darling, the longer you leave it, the more likely he'll think he *is*,' said Mum. 'I was going out with this boy once—'

'Okay, okay,' I said hastily, to cut off her reminiscences of Great Losers of History. 'You really think I should ring him now?'

'We'll wait for you.'

'No! Don't – you go, and I'll bike round to Anna's when I'm finished.'

'What? What's Jem doing? If she's only making a phone call—' Dad was not quite with it as usual.

'Come round when you're ready, darling,' said Mum.

They left. Mum was still trying to explain the situation to Dad, though given I'd hardly told her anything, it was a miracle she understood as much as she did. But mothers are amazing; they have freakish powers. I waited till the car was gone, then I took the phone into my room.

I knew Mum was right; I'd have to be firm. I felt sick.

'Hello?'

It was Bec; I felt even sicker. 'Oh, hi – it's me.'

'Jem, hi! Did you want to speak to me or Richard?' She sounded horribly coy. I felt as if I was holding a machete over the head of a poor little lamb.

Richard came to the phone, very jovial. 'Hello, hello, Jem, how are you?'

'Good, yeah, good,' I said.

There was a pause, then we both started speaking at once.

'Sorry, after you.'

'No, you go first.'

Richard took a deep breath. 'I was just going to say how glad I am that you called, in fact – that we can—'

This was getting worse. And knowing Bec was probably hovering in the background didn't help. I had to stop him.

'Listen, Richard, this is – I've got something to say, and it's a bit awkward, but – I can't think of a good way to tell you . . .' Yeah, *that* was the right thing to say. I was handling this *so well*. I blurted out, 'I don't think it's a good idea for us to see each other any more.'

There was silence on the other end of the line. I had all my arguments ready: I was too young, I had to concentrate on school, I wasn't ready to go out with anyone et cetera, et cetera. But he cut me off.

'I see,' he said, very coldly.

'I just don't think——'

'I'm very disappointed, in fact. You haven't given yourself a chance to get to know me. We've only been out together twice.'

'Three times,' I said faintly.

'So, you made up your mind about me after a blink of an eye?' His voice rose. 'I'm surprised, I didn't think you were so shallow. I'm very disappointed. I tried to make sure you had a good time. I was not very interested in that exhibition, in fact. I went because you said you wanted to. And now you don't want to see me again. Is that fair? I don't think so.'

This was torture. Harriet Vane had a thousand elegant ways of refusing Peter Wimsey's attentions, and of course I couldn't think of one. But then, underneath, she liked him all along. Well, that was one question resolved. I didn't like Richard Patel *at all*.

'I'm sorry,' I said. 'I just don't . . . I'm not ready to . . . I'm really sorry.' My heart was pumping hard and my hands were clammy.

'You're sorry? I see. Then everything is all right, in fact.' Apparently Bec wasn't the only member of the family to get sarcastic when she was angry.

But I was almost glad he was so angry. Every second that passed I was surer I'd made the right decision. 'I'm sorry, Richard. Thank you for taking me to the exhibition, I had a good—'

He hung up. I stared at the phone. No one had ever hung up on me before. 'Hello?' I said stupidly, but he'd gone.

I sat holding the phone. My knees were shaking. I'd been prepared for him to be hurt, to try and talk me out of it. But I didn't expect him to *lose* it.

I thought, too late, of things I could have said: that I hadn't wanted to go to the stupid exhibition either; that he shouldn't have tried to kiss me; that I'd only gone out with him in the first place because I didn't realise it was a date. Why did he ring me and ask me out again after I'd practically pushed him off me? What kind of an idiot was he?

I felt as if my head was going to burst. I had to talk about this to someone. If Mum had been home, I would have poured it all out to her, but I was shy about telling the whole story in front of Anna. Anna was so cool. Anna would never have had an awkward moment with a boy, not even in the days when she still went out with them.

I could ring Bec.

Idiot. Bec was going to be *so* sympathetic. It just shows how shaken up I was, that I even considered ringing her.

Then I thought of Mackenzie. Mackenzie, who knew all about boys. She was the perfect person to talk to.

My heart beat faster than ever. Okay, she didn't want to hang out with me at school. But maybe it would be okay if I called her at home. After all, this was an emergency.

Without letting myself think about it, I punched in her number.

Her mobile was switched off.

I still had a chance to save my self-respect. I ignored it. I dialled her home number. It wasn't too late; while it was ringing, I could still have hung up, no one would ever know—

'Hello?'

'Hello, Mrs Woodrow? Could I please speak to Mackenzie?'

'Mackenzie isn't here, I'm afraid.'

'Oh. Okay—' I was about to say, *never mind*, and hang up.

But Mackenzie's mum said, 'You might find her down at the Boot Factory, you know, where the cinemas are? They've gone for ice-creams.'

'Oh, right. Thanks.' She didn't need to know I'd rather cut off my finger than track down Mackenzie and her little gang at an ice-cream shop.

She didn't ask who I was; I didn't leave a message. Phew.

Mackenzie would never know I'd rung. My self-respect was saved. Despite my best efforts.

I called Iris. At least I knew she'd be home; she was always home.

'Something terrible's happened.'

'What?'

'I had to dump Bec's brother.'

For a second Iris said nothing, then, quite coolly, 'I wasn't aware that you were . . . together.'

'Well, we weren't really, I guess. But we did go out on a couple of dates, then he asked me out again and I had to say I wasn't interested.'

Again the cool silence. Iris was so the wrong person to talk to about this, I realised; she was much more fascinated by fictional relationships than real ones. She could talk about Wimscy and Harriet, or Captain Pinker and Wolf, for hours on end, but not boy–girl relationships in the real world. She said, 'Hang on a sec.' There was a muted noise in the background, then she picked up again.

'Do you think you've broken his heart?'

'Of course not! It was just . . . awkward.' Now I felt like an idiot. As if anyone would be heartbroken at the prospect of not going on a date with *me*. It was laughable. I said, 'But it's Bec's brother. What am I going to say to Bec?'

'Hang on,' she said, and covered the phone again.

I hung on, picking at a thread on my doona.

'Sorry,' said Iris. 'I'm here.'

'I just wish I could wind back time. I wish I'd never gone on the stupid dates. I can't go out with him just because he's my friend's brother—' I heard a muffled beep in the background, and broke off. 'Iris, are you texting?'

Silence. 'Mm – no.'

Iris is a worse liar than I am. 'Is it Bec? What's she say?'

'Gotta go,' said Iris hastily. '*Starfield 5*'s on in a minute. I'll call you later.'

'Thanks for your support,' I said.

'That's okay,' said Iris, choosing to ignore my sarcasm. Then *she* hung up on me too.

I was *sure* she and Bec were texting. Bec must have got hold of a mobile. What was she saying? I chewed my fingernails.

Then I decided. Damn it. I would go to the Boot Factory. It was only eight o'clock (half an hour till *Starfield 5*, Iris, by the way; check the clock before you lie to me next time.) It was only ten minutes on the bike, and I could ride to Anna's afterwards. Maybe I just felt like a pre-dinner ice-cream.

I thought Mackenzie would probably be gone by the time I got there. How long does it take to eat an ice-cream? I knew the Boot Factory, of course, but I never hung out there. It was a place where golden people hung out, not nerds . . . There was a giant bookshop there, though. I could pretend I was going to buy a book. That was a reasonable nerdy alibi.

I chained the bike to a no-parking sign and tried to look nonchalant as I strolled inside the huge, garish, echoing shopping mall that had once been a place where poor people stitched boots together. I walked slowly toward the entrance to the bookshop, swinging my bike helmet (that must have looked cool) and glancing around casually in the direction of the ice-cream shop.

There were a few people sitting at tables outside the shop; no sign of Mackenzie or any of her crowd. They must have gone already . . .

Then I saw her.

She was examining the bookshop window display, holding an ice-cream cone. Gelato, of course; nothing fattening for Mackenzie Woodrow.

She was with a boy.

He was a tall, blond-haired boy with a narrow, handsome face and excellent cheekbones. For a second I thought he might be Mackenzie's long-lost brother, because they looked so much alike. But no. They were holding hands.

I felt as if someone had punched me in the chest. I couldn't breathe; I had to turn away.

I ducked inside the entrance and practically galloped to the back of the store where I hid between two shelves. I picked up a book and blindly turned the pages.

Mackenzie had a boyfriend.

Who was he? How did they meet? How long had this

been going on? She'd told me she didn't have a boyfriend. Had she lied to me, or was he a recent acquisition? Was that why? But that didn't make sense . . . Did Mackenzie – I dunno – did she *love* him? Had they kissed? Had they done more than that? Was that why she hadn't told me, because she knew I wouldn't understand, because I was just a naive child who was too scared even to kiss a boy?

My throat was tight. I blinked at the book and suddenly my eyes cleared and I saw that I was holding a sex manual. I nearly dropped it; then I peeped, very quickly, at the page that was open. I'd never realised human beings could bend like that . . . I filed the information away for a different lifetime, shoved the book back onto the shelf and walked away, fast.

Mackenzie had a boyfriend.

Did she think I'd disapprove?

Actually, I did disapprove. In fact, as Richard Patel would say.

Oh, the irony. If I rang Richard and apologised, was it too late for me to have a boyfriend too?

When I emerged from the bookshop Mackenzie and her paramour had disappeared, and it was dark outside. I hardly noticed the streets as I rode; I pedalled home on automatic pilot. I forgot I was supposed to be going to Anna's.

Mackenzie had a boyfriend.

There were always boys underfoot, she'd said. She'd

said she'd tell me. Did she think I'd be jealous? Maybe she'd rushed out and got this boy to show me I wasn't the only one who could pull a guy.

'Jessica Martinic,' I told myself. 'You're losing it.' I tried to sound firm, but my voice was wobbly.

When Mum and Dad got home I was in the kitchen eating chips in the dark.

'What's this?' said Dad. 'Are you all right?'

'Ssh,' said Mum. 'She's all right.'

'It would have been polite to call Anna,' said Dad.

'It's all right,' said Mum. 'It didn't matter.' I could see she was dying to ask me how it went; she was *heroically* holding back.

'Everything's fine,' I said. 'But I'm very tired. I think I'll go to bed.'

I lay awake for a long time. Harriet Vane was *twenty-eight* before Lord Peter came along. If I had to face another *twelve years* of this, I'd die, simple as that.

And in the morning, I had to face Bec.

Maybe I was wrong about Iris texting her. Maybe Richard wouldn't tell her anything . . . But I'm no Mackenzie Woodrow (I wish *she* wouldn't keep popping up) – I can't act to save my life. Bec was going to know something was wrong the second she laid eyes on me.

Or maybe not. Bec was terrible at picking up social signals. You practically had to beat her over the head to get her to notice things that other people sensed without a word. If Iris hadn't been texting, if Richard didn't tell her, she'd never know. The whole thing would just evaporate like morning mist.

I kept telling myself that, and finally I fell asleep.

Forget about Bec laying eyes on me. I only had to lay eyes on *her* to see that she knew everything.

I swallowed. 'Hi, Bec.'

'Hi.' Lips pressed together, frown, quick look away.

'Bec . . . You know, I really *like* Richard — I mean, he's lovely—'

'Yeah, I know he is.'

'Bec . . .'

'It's okay, Jem. You don't have to say anything.' She gave me a tight little smile and withdrew.

I grabbed Georgia. 'George, George, can you do me a favour?'

'Yeah . . . Right now? I just need to run over to the PE Centre . . .'

'I'll come with you.'

We fell into step. 'Georgia, can you talk to Bec for me? Can you tell her that I think her brother's really nice, but we're just not compatible? No, don't say that. Tell her I'm really sorry, but I'm not ready to go out with anyone at the moment . . .'

'Wow,' said Georgia. 'Did you dump him?'

'No — yes — kind of.'

'No wonder Bec's so pissed off.'

'Is she? With me? Did she say that?'

'I'll find out,' said Georgia reassuringly. 'I'll get back to you.'

In assembly, Iris and Bec sat together, and Georgia and I sat in the row behind. Afterwards Georgia and Iris conferred for a few minutes, then Georgia ran back to me.

'Richard thinks you dumped him because he's Indian. Because you don't want to go out with a black boy.'

'*What?* That's crazy!' I laughed in disbelief, which was a big mistake, because Bec turned and saw me. Her face froze in a mask of fury, and she grabbed Iris by the arm and marched off across the quad. Iris grimaced at me, and pantomimed that she'd catch up with me later, and we'd sort this whole mess out. Either that or something in her pants was biting her.

I said, 'Bec *knows* I'm not racist.'

Georgia shrugged. 'Richard told Bec you felt weird about dating an Indian boy.'

'That's *insane*! Why would he say that? Bec must have got the wrong end of the stick again. I felt weird about dating *him*, but it's nothing to do with being Indian! Bec's been my best friend since forever — and Iris. And you, of course,' I added hastily, since Georgia was looking a little hurt. 'Sheesh, George, I've got plenty of flaws, but racism isn't one of them. Bec never even calls herself Indian!

She's as Aussie as I am! It's like Iris calling herself Chinese.'

'She's not Chinese. She's Malaysian.'

'No, she's Chinese. Isn't she?'

'Her family come from Malaysia.'

'But they're Chinese, aren't they?'

'I don't know.'

I threw my hands in the air. '*Iris* is a bigger racist than I am.'

'What do you mean?'

'She wants to be English.'

'Anglo? No, she doesn't.'

'No, not Anglo, *English*. Oxford and cricket and Lord Peter Wimsey English.'

'But English isn't a race. Anglo's a race. If she wants to be English, it's not being racist. Is it? Is Anglo a race?'

'I don't know!'

'So what are we arguing about?'

'We're not arguing!'

'Okay!'

I really didn't want to start a fight with Georgia as well. The whole thing made my brain hurt. Indian, Croatian, Chinese, Anglo, I'd never given it much thought, but suddenly everything was an ethnic conflict. No wonder it was so hard to make peace in the Middle East.

'Do you think I need a nose job?' asked Georgia suddenly.

I stared at her. 'Can we focus, please?'

Georgia touched her nose, frowning cross-eyed. 'Seriously.'

'No, I don't think you need a nose job.'

Georgia let go of her nose. 'Don't worry. I've got Maths with Iris now. I'll sort it out.'

They were still sorting it out at recess in our corner of the quad, so I went for a walk. Just an aimless kind of walk, round the back of the Music School to the little courtyard where our gang used to hang out last year. There was no one there; no new group of Year 9s had adopted it, which was a shame, because it was a great spot — sunny, but sheltered. I sat on the bench and stirred the gravel with my foot and thought about how pleasant it would be to go back to the simple, uncomplicated world of Year 9.

'Hi.'

I nearly jumped out of my skin. Mackenzie Woodrow had materialised beside me. She was alone. We were alone.

I didn't say anything. My heart was thudding in my chest.

She said, 'I heard about you and Bec.'

I still didn't say anything.

'Rosie told me, she got it from Georgia. They hang out, you know.'

I stared over the top of the wall, down the slope toward the Junior School. I had nothing to say.

Mackenzie said softly, 'I saw you last night. At the Boot Factory.'

I darted a look at her, before I could stop myself. She was gazing straight ahead.

'His name's Ted. He's from St Andrew's, he's in Year 11. He's on the debating team, that's how we met. He was just, kind of . . . perfect.'

I didn't say anything, but I felt my jaw clenching tighter.

'He's a lovely guy,' said Mackenzie. 'You'd like him.'

I was going to speak; my breath came fast. I was getting ready to do it; all the words were bunched up in my throat. I just had to swallow so I could get them out.

Mackenzie said softly, 'I'm sorry, Jem.'

She stood up, and before I could open my mouth she was gone.

When the bell rang, I made my way back to the quad; Bec and Iris and Georgia were still there, huddled together. I stood near the lockers, waiting for them.

Georgia was first; she sidled over, looking harassed.

'Is it sorted?' I said.

Georgia shifted from foot to foot. 'Not exactly.'

Then Bec and Iris came in. Bec threw a glare at me with the force of a hand grenade. Iris didn't even glance in my direction. She banged open her locker, banged it shut, and marched away down the corridor. If she'd been a dog, she would have bristled.

'Georgia, what happened?'

'I'm working on it.' Georgia screwed her face up.

'What's up with Iris? Georgia, you didn't — you didn't tell her what I said about—'

'It kind of . . . slipped out. I was just telling Bec what you said, about not being racist . . .'

I groaned. '*Georgia!*'

'I'll fix it, I'll fix it.'

'I'll talk to them myself.'

'Jem, I don't think that's a good idea. They're pretty upset.'

Rosie Lee slouched up and draped herself against the lockers. 'Got a spare?' she said to Georgia. She completely ignored me.

'Yeah,' said Georgia. 'But—' She glanced at me. In the spare before English we usually went to the library together.

'Want to get some early lunch? I'm soooo hungry.'

Georgia peeped at me again. We both knew what Rosie meant; she was going to sneak out of the grounds and up the road to the fast food place. Strictly forbidden, of course. Heaps of trouble if you got caught. In all my years at school I'd never done it once. Neither, as far as I knew, had Georgia.

Now she said slowly, 'Well.. . .'

Rosie Lee flicked a glance at me and curled her lip. 'She won't rat on us. Will you, Jem?'

I felt myself go red. 'I wouldn't dream of it.'

'I wouldn't dream of it,' mimicked Rosie, and laughed. Georgia stared at her shoes, but she was smiling.

'Do what you like,' I said shortly, and walked off down the corridor toward the library. At the stairs I loitered for a minute or two, but Georgia didn't catch me up, and when I looked back, she and Rosie had vanished.

june

I'd never really thought about it before, how important friends are. Obviously, without exactly analysing the details, I knew they were important, in the same way that eating is important, and sleep is important. But now I realised how much of *me* was determined by who my friends were. And if my friends suddenly weren't there any more, who was I? I'd lost my context; I was losing myself. I didn't mind being invisible, but not ceasing to exist.

Of course I wanted to talk to them. Maybe Georgia was right, maybe it was too soon. But I hated the idea of not being friends; I couldn't stand it. Not on top of the whole Mackenzie thing. Okay, so I'd stuffed things up with Mackenzie, but these guys were my *true* friends. We weren't going to break up over a paltry misunderstanding like this.

At lunchtime there was no sign of Georgia. So I marched up to Bec and Iris, who were sitting in the corner of the quad – our corner, the dank, sunless corner under the weird wall-statue of the girl and the dog – and I took a deep breath, and I said, 'I'm really, really sorry.'

Bec and Iris didn't look at each other, but a telepathic buzz seemed to run between them. Bec said, in a completely alien, polite voice, 'That's okay, Jem.'

'Really?'

'Sure.'

I said to Iris, 'I don't know what Georgia told you exactly, but you know I didn't mean anything bad.'

'Of course not,' said Iris, also very politely.

'So everything's okay? We're still friends?'

'Of course we are,' said Bec.

I hesitated for a second, then I sat down. No one said anything. I took out my lunch and unwrapped my sandwich. Iris muttered something to Bec, and she laughed.

'What?'

Bec waved her hand. 'Nothing, nothing.'

I bit into my sandwich. Bec and Iris ate their lunches in silence.

I said, 'Anyone want one of my nana's biscuits?'

'No, thanks,' said Iris politely.

'No, thanks,' said Bec. 'Unless – they're not short-breads, are they?'

Iris exploded into laughter, and stifled it behind her hand. Bec smiled, as if she was trying not to, but couldn't help it.

I smiled too. 'What's the joke?'

Bec and Iris exchanged glances. Bec said, 'Nothing, never mind.' So this was a *private* joke. Just for the two of them.

'Okay,' I said, still smiling. 'Okay.'

It was like being surrounded by invisible walls. And it hurt, every day. It didn't get any better, though it wasn't quite so bad when Georgia was there. It was weird. Anyone who saw us would say we were still friends: we hung out together, we caught the bus together, we ate lunch together, we sat together in class. On the surface, nothing had changed. But under the surface, everything was different.

It was confusing. Part of me just felt sad. I would have done anything to put things back the way they were. I would have got down on my knees and apologised, even though I didn't think I had anything to apologise for. But I *had* apologised, and it hadn't made a scrap of difference. What more could I do?

And part of me was pissed off, more than anything. Bec was driving me nuts. I was annoyed with Iris for taking offence and not admitting it, and for being on Bec's side all the time. And Georgia — I love Georgia, I've always loved Georgia, but . . . we're not on the same wavelength. Georgia and I don't quite *get* each other the way Iris did, the way Bec did. The way Mackenzie did.

And Georgia wasn't always there. She was hanging round more and more with Rosie Lee, especially since Georgia took the great leap forward into the party scene. Nothing bad had happened, yet – though I got the impression Georgia didn't always give us a full report. She and Rosie Lee huddled together in corners, whispering, with Georgia nodding earnestly. She wasn't in the gang, as such, Mackenzie's gang, but sometimes I suspected that was what Rosie was grooming her for. I let myself wonder, just briefly, how I'd feel if Georgia became friends with Mackenzie. I decided I'd have to kill her.

Joking. Of course. But actually, deep down, it didn't feel like a joke, and I had to push that feeling away.

For the first morning in weeks, Iris caught the early bus with me, instead of the later one with Bec and Georgia.

'Hi.' She gave me an awkward smile. 'Mind if I sit down?'

'Sure . . .' I shifted to make room.

'How did you go with that French translation? Wasn't it a *killer*?'

'Killer,' I echoed.

'You couldn't give me a hand with it, could you?'

'Um, okay.'

It wasn't like Iris to ask for help. This was the friendliest overture she'd made since the Rift had opened between us. But for some reason her chumminess was making me anxious; it felt as if she was preparing an ambush.

'So,' she said, as we strolled up the school drive. 'You coming to the meeting today?'

I blinked. 'What meeting?'

'The meeting about the International Baccalaureate.'

'Oh – yeah,' I said slowly.

'We should find out about it, don't you think? Much better chance of getting into Oxford with an IB score.' There was a pause. 'So, are you coming?'

I shifted my bag to the other shoulder. 'Um . . . I don't think I am.'

'Not coming to the meeting, or not coming to Oxford?'

'Not coming to Oxford.'

'Right,' said Iris. 'I see.'

'I didn't realise you were serious.'

'Of course I'm serious. I thought you were serious, too. You always sounded serious.'

'I guess I've changed my mind,' I said. 'I think I want to be an editor.'

Iris pulled a face. 'Well, you can study *that* anywhere.'

'Not quite anywhere. But I don't have to go to Oxford.'

'Okay,' said Iris after a minute. 'I guess I'll go by myself then.'

'It wasn't ever, you know, a cast-iron agreement or

anything. I didn't *promise*. I thought we were just joking around.'

Iris didn't say anything.

'I'm sorry, Iris.'

'That's okay. You've got to do what you've got to do.'

'Yeah,' I said.

She flipped her hand, as if to say, no worries, and then she sped up and vanished into the library without looking back. I watched her go. Part of me was surprised that she really did intend to try for Oxford after all, and part of me was slightly regretful; going to England with Iris would have been fun.

But *Oxford* — it was absurd, it was a dream. Our image of Oxford was stuck in the 1930s; it wasn't real, and I didn't think Iris would find what she was looking for if she went there. It was a fantasy, like our crush on Lord Peter Wimsey was a fantasy. We both knew that was a game, and planning Oxford had been a game, too.

Only not for Iris. I wondered why we'd never really had this conversation before. And I wondered, now the illusion had been shattered, if that spelled the end for Iris and me. Things were so shaky anyway; take away Oxford, and Peter Wimsey, and cricket, and rolling our eyes at Bec, and there wasn't a whole lot left to hold our friendship together.

And now she had one more reason to feel like I'd let her down . . .

As if we could have gone to Oxford. We would have driven each other crazy.

'Could all Year 10s stay back for a few moments after assembly, please?'

We coughed and shuffled as everyone else filed out under cover of the organ blasting from the gallery overhead, and then abruptly the music stopped and Ms Wells stepped up to the lectern.

'Now, girls, I have an exciting opportunity to share with you.'

Beside me Iris groaned softly to Bec.

'Unfortunately those of you who are taking part in the concert at the end of next term will *not* be able to participate in this event. I'm very sorry, but it was impossible to change the schedule. But for the rest of Year 10, I am happy to announce that I have organised for us all to share a unique opportunity to hear Charles Le Tan speak. I'm sure you're all as excited as I am—' She held up a hand for quiet.

Iris muttered, 'Who the devil?'

Bec whispered in her ear and Iris leaned toward her and whispered back.

Behind me I heard Mackenzie Woodrow's clear, low voice. 'He's an inspirational speaker. Like the Dalai Lama.'

'The Dalai Lama?' Georgia squeaked.

'I said *like* the Dalai Lama,' corrected Mackenzie. 'At

least, he thinks he is.' I didn't turn around, but I could just imagine her cool, amused smile.

'Quiet, girls, please!' called Ms Wells. 'As you're probably aware, Charles Le Tan is making one appearance only in Australia, so we will be travelling to Sydney to hear him speak.'

Major buzz of excitement.

'This trip is being organised in conjunction with St Andrew's College, which means—' She was practically shouting now; girls bounced in their seats. 'We will be flying up together and sharing accommodation.'

Several people squealed. Not Mackenzie. But I'm sure she was squealing on the inside.

'Girls, *please*. We will be on separate floors of the hotel and any *inappropriate* behaviour will be *severely punished*. Does everybody understand?' She frowned at us sternly. 'Permission forms will go home *today*. I need them back by *next Wednesday*, so we can finalise numbers. If there are any questions, come and see me at lunchtime, *not* now.'

There was a cacophony of banging seats as everyone stood up at once. I saw Mackenzie turn away; she was staring at the floor. I would have expected her to be rapt at the prospect of a trip to Sydney with her St Andrew's sweetheart, but she didn't seem happy. Then I remembered. Of course Mackenzie wasn't squealing on the inside. She'd be reading poetry at the concert; she couldn't go. Hooray.

It rained at lunchtime so we were stuck inside.

Georgia said, 'The Sydney trip costs a thousand dollars.'

'*What?*' I said.

Bec reached for another sandwich. 'The tickets for Le Tan must cost at least that much. With accommodation and flights and trips to the galleries and whatever else they're planning on the side, it's extremely cheap, in fact.'

I'd never noticed that Bec said 'in fact', like her damned and blasted brother. But now I did notice and it was driving me insane.

I said, 'For Pete's sake, how ridiculous. There are plenty of things I'd rather spend a thousand bucks on than hearing some paltry so-called inspirational speaker.'

'I have to save up for Oxford,' said Iris gloomily. She shot a quick glance at me, but I refused to feel guilty. 'But I guess I'll go if you guys go.'

'*Charles Le Tan,*' I snorted. 'I've heard he's a complete idiot.'

'Yeah?' said Bec. 'Where did you hear that?'

'Mackenzie—' I stopped myself, too late.

'Oh, well, if *Mackenzie* says it, it must be true.'

Bec had always been sarcastic. She hadn't got any more sarcastic lately. But now it was always directed at me. Iris laughed. Bec was *so* hilarious.

'It's a lot of money,' said Georgia quietly.

Rosie Lee was sitting on the other side of the room with Phillipa and Jessica Samuels and Frances. I don't know where Mackenzie was; concert rehearsal, probably. But suddenly Rosie oozed over to us and draped her arm around Georgia's shoulders.

'What's up, Georgia? Can't your mum afford to send you to Sydney?'

Rosie's voice was super-sympathetic, but there was the faintest twist to her mouth, and she raised an eyebrow at the rest of her gang, who were perched on the bench top. Predictably, Frances and Phillipa tittered.

Georgia sat very still. 'We'll manage,' she said uncertainly.

'Course you will,' cooed Rosie. 'You're so brave, Georgia. I love this girl,' she announced to the crowded room. 'She never complains. Just check out her shoes.'

Involuntarily we all looked at Georgia's cracked and scuffed shoes. She tucked her feet under her chair and her face went pink. She said in a small voice, 'I'm getting new shoes next term.'

Rosie kissed the side of her head. 'Listen to her, will you? Never whinges, never asks for help . . . I know!' She swung around to include the whole of Lab 5. 'Let's take up a collection to help Georgia get to Sydney!'

'Get lost, Rosie,' I said. 'Georgia doesn't need your help.'

'Mind your own business, Martinic,' said Rosie. 'You want Georgia to be left behind? Come on guys, get your wallets out – give generously! Georgia Harris deserves a trip to Sydney. Let's help her out!'

'I'll put in ten dollars!' called Phillipa, waving her money aloft.

'I'll put in twenty!' yelled Frances.

The room erupted in laughter and catcalls as people pulled out their money like it was the best joke ever. Someone threw Rosie an ice-cream container and she danced around the lab shaking it as people tossed money in. Georgia's face was scarlet.

'Give generously to the Georgia Harris Appeal!' shouted Rosie, and when she'd been all around the room she headed for the door.

'She's going to go right round the school!' I said in horror. 'We've got to stop her!'

Bec and Iris just stared at me as if I'd suggested standing in front of a cyclone.

Georgia grabbed my sleeve. 'Leave it, Jem, you'll only make it worse.' Her eyes were full of tears. '*Please.*'

'Anyway, she's gone,' said Iris flatly.

We could hear Rosie's voice echoing down the corridor. 'Georgia Harris Appeal – give that she may go!'

'It's just a joke,' said Georgia faintly. 'She's only trying to help.'

I stared at her. Georgia never talked about it, but we all knew it was a struggle for her mum to afford the fees. And yes, she did buy her textbooks at the second-hand book sale, and yes, her uniform was shabbier than everyone else's. But our families, Bec's and Iris's and mine, we thought twice before we spent money. We weren't poor – certainly not compared to most people in the world, who had to get by without clean water or fresh food or even a roof over their heads. If Iris and I weren't on scholarships, we'd probably have bought our uniforms at the swap shop too.

Compared to Rosie and Frances and Mackenzie and that crowd, with their holiday houses and their yachts and their skiing trips and their shopping sprees in Bangkok, yeah, we were not silver-spoon-in-our-mouths rich, and Rosie prancing around the corridors shaking her collection box was an attempt to humiliate us all.

I pushed back my chair and slipped off to the library alone, which seemed to be my natural state these days. So I wasn't in the lab when Rosie returned – trailing a parade of giggling followers behind her – and presented Georgia with the money, to wild applause and whooping. Georgia took it; what else could she do?

She was supposed to have Biology that afternoon, but she wagged it to track me down in the library; I had a double spare.

'Look,' she hissed, and showed me her bulging pencil case. 'What am I going to do?'

'How much is there?'

'I don't know.'

I propped up my folder and we counted it. Georgia whispered, 'It's about three hundred and forty dollars.'

'You can't keep it.'

'I'm not going to keep it! But I can't give it back, can I?' Georgia glanced anxiously around the library. 'Everybody's laughing at me.'

'Bloody Rosie. Viper-cow.'

'She meant well – no, she did, Jem. She was just joking and it got out of hand, that's all. It's not her fault – you should hear how her father upsets her. She's just acting out, she can't help it.'

'Oh, please. I can't believe you're defending her,' I hissed. I zipped up the pencil case. 'Come on.'

'Where are we going?'

'We're going to give it to Mrs Dyson.' Mrs Dyson was in charge of the social service collection. 'She'll be rapt.'

'But – what are we going to tell her?'

'Tell her you raised it for refugees. She'll think you're a saint.'

'But – it's not true. Rosie raised it, she should get the credit.'

'Rosie Lee—' I took a deep breath. 'When will you get it through your thick skull that Rosie was making fun of you? She *can* help it, and she wasn't being *nice*!'

Georgia held out her hand for the pencil case and her voice wobbled. 'I'll take it myself. You think what you like. But I know . . . I know I'm special to Rosie. She doesn't want me to miss out on going to Sydney.'

I gave up. 'All right, whatever. Tell Mrs Dyson that Rosie's a refugee advocate now. See if she believes you.'

It worked out pretty well in the end, better than I could have hoped. Georgia did tell Mrs Dyson that Rosie had raised the money for refugees, but was too shy to take the credit, and Mrs Dyson was so impressed she announced to the whole school that Rosie would have to put her talents to good use and join the social work committee. Just the thought of Rosie Lee on the social work committee was so gobsmackingly wrong it cheered me up for a week.

One day at recess little Sonia Darcy came up to me in the corridor and whispered in my ear. 'Mackenzie Woodrow wants to see you.'

I stared at her. 'I beg your pardon?'

'She's outside the Music School. She said you'd know where.'

The universe throws us gifts. I shut my laptop into my locker. No one was waiting for me; Bec and Iris had disappeared and Georgia had gone off on some errand for Rosie. I tried to summon up the proper outrage: who did Mackenzie Woodrow think she was, commanding me to her presence? And why not just come up and talk to me? What was with all this *skulduggery*? (No one knows where that word comes from. It must be something to do with digging up corpses, though, surely.)

Anyway I tried to be furious, but I couldn't. What I mostly felt was curiosity and, well, excitement at the thought of seeing her. Pathetic, I know.

'Hi.'

'Hi.'

She was sitting on the bench. I stood in front of her, but then it felt like an interview, so I sat down. And that way I couldn't see her face; it was easier.

'We haven't got much time,' she said.

'You recruiting for ASIO?'

I think she smiled. 'I wanted to talk to you about something.'

I tried to keep my voice as cool as hers. 'What about?'

'Georgia Harris and Rosie.'

'What about them?'

'I've been watching them. I don't think they've got a very healthy relationship.'

I couldn't have agreed more; I'd been watching them too. But now for some reason all the fury I'd tried to conjure earlier built up inside me. My voice went cold. 'What do you want me to do about it?'

'Can't you talk to Georgia?'

'Why should I talk to Georgia? She's the victim! Why don't you talk to Rosie?'

'Georgia hangs around with Rosie making goo-goo eyes; she's like a puppy. It's too pathetic.'

'Well,' I said. 'I never believed you could be such a cow.'

'I'm sorry,' said Mackenzie at once. She swung around and seized my hand. 'I shouldn't have said that. I didn't mean it, I'm sorry.'

I shook her hand off mine. 'Don't – *act* at me.'

There was silence. Mackenzie folded her hands in her lap. At last she said in a strangled voice, 'I'm sorry, all right? What else can I say? But I'm worried. I don't know what to do. Rosie's getting into a bad scene and I can't stop her. She won't listen to me. She's too busy showing Georgia how *cool* she is.'

'I don't know what Georgia and I can do. You can't expect the victim to control the bully.'

'You think Rosie's bullying Georgia?'

'Well – yeah. Don't you?'

For a minute Mackenzie was quiet. Then she said, 'If you really think Georgia's being bullied, shouldn't you tell someone?'

For the first time I looked her square in the face. Slowly I said, 'Is that why you got me here? Because you're too gutless to report Rosie, and you want me to do your dirty work?'

Mackenzie's big blue eyes met mine for a second, then she dropped her gaze. 'I think Rosie needs help. But if I did anything – she'd never forgive me.'

I shook my head. 'It's none of my business.'

'But Georgia's your friend. I thought you believed in – I dunno, protecting the meek and standing up for the powerless?'

'What am I, Robin Hood?'

'That was your idea, the refugee donation, wasn't it?

I knew that was you: Georgia Harris couldn't think up a scheme like that. That was smart, brilliant.'

'Don't, Mackenzie! Don't – smarm up to me.'

Silence again. 'I'm not,' said Mackenzie coldly. 'I just thought you were the kind of person who stood by their friends. I must have been wrong. I'm disappointed, that's all.'

I let out a breath. 'How can *you* sit there and lecture *me* about the importance of friendship after the way you behaved? How *dare* you. Are you stupid? Or was *our* friendship so paltry to you that you've forgotten?'

Mackenzie turned her head away.

'Unbelievable,' I said. I stood up. My knees were shaking. 'How's your boyfriend?'

'He's good.'

'Great. I'm so pleased.'

'So are you going to report the bullying?' she said, without looking at me.

'*No.*'

But I knew I would do something. And I knew Mackenzie knew it too.

june

Our school has a bullying policy, of course. But I've never seen it put into action. There was a big fuss about it when we started Year 7; we had pamphlets to take home and a two-hour session on bully-proofing ourselves, but since then, nada. Maybe we were all so effectively bully-proofed on that day there was no need to mention it again. Except Georgia's armour seemed to have cracked, with help from Rosie who was expertly skewering her in all the right places.

I was still contemplating the best way to tackle this delicate situation when one recess a few days later I saw an email Rosie had sent to Georgia. It was a link to a website that advertised diet pills.

'George, what is this?'

Georgia turned bright red. 'Nothing.'

'Why would Rosie send you this?'

'She sends me stuff all the time.'

'Stuff like this? *Fat* stuff?'

'*No*. Other stuff too, lots of things . . .'

Suddenly I remembered something. 'Did she say you needed a nose job?'

'She didn't say I *needed* one . . .'

'But she sent you a link?'

Georgia said nothing, but her hand crept up to her nose.

'Right, that's it.' I grabbed my books and my laptop and stood up.

'Where are you going? The bell's about to ring.'

'I don't care,' I said over my shoulder, and as I marched away I glimpsed Mackenzie, in the middle of her gaggle. Though I didn't look at her directly, I saw her eyes follow me as I went by, and I admit I felt a warm glow of self-righteousness, an essence of Robin Hood-ish rebel bravado bubbling through my veins.

I marched straight to the counsellor's office. The bell rang as I got there.

'I need to see Ms Wells. It's urgent.'

Maybe the counsellor's secretary thought I was going to kill myself or, even more serious, drop Maths, because she sent me straight in. Ms Wells gave me a plastic smile.

'Jessica, isn't it? What can I do for you?'

Ms Wells is the only person in the universe who doesn't call me Jem.

'I'd like to report a case of bullying.'

Ms Wells's face instantly snapped into no-laughing-matter mode. 'I see.' She shut the door. 'You'd better sit down. This is a very serious accusation, Jessica. Who has been bullying you?'

'Oh, it's not me. It's Georgia Harris. She's being bullied. By Rosie Lee.'

At the mention of Rosie's name, Ms Wells' expression underwent a subtle and unreadable shift. I figured that Rosie must be a frequent customer in the counselling department, due to the difficult home life we were always hearing so much about. Ms Wells must know a lot about Rosie.

'I see. And why isn't Georgia with you?'

'I didn't − I didn't tell her I was coming.' Which did sound feeble, I admit.

'So you've taken it upon yourself to report this alleged behaviour on Georgia's behalf?'

'Well − yes, I guess so.'

'And what is the behaviour, exactly?'

'Rosie sends her emails for diet pills and plastic surgery and she makes her go to parties. And she − looks at her . . .'

'Rosie invites Georgia to parties? And she *looks* at her?'

'Yes.'

Ms Wells frowned at me. I felt helpless. Anyone else

would have understood what I meant; any girl in the school would have known. The poison looks that slid sideways across the classroom or the corridor or the quad; the stifled laugh, the sly smile, the whisper. Georgia's uncertain smile back, her hopeful, pleading smile . . . I knew exactly what it felt like. Bec and Iris had been doing it to me for weeks – except they were my friends; Rosie wasn't a friend to Georgia, not really and truly . . .

'Rosie makes jokes about her,' I said in a rush. 'You remember when Rosie raised money for the refugees? Well, she didn't raise it for refugees, she raised it for Georgia – she took up a collection so Georgia could go on the Sydney trip, to hear Charles Le Tan – Georgia's mum doesn't have much money . . .'

'Rosie collected money for Georgia. And you interpret this as bullying behaviour?'

'It *was*. She was being mean, she was trying to humiliate Georgia, not help her.'

Ms Wells stood up. 'I'm sorry, Jessica, but unless Georgia is prepared to substantiate what you say, I really can't act on what you've told me.'

It was hopeless; Ms Wells just didn't get it. She never would; she was on Rosie's side. I said desperately, 'Well, can we get Georgia in here?'

Ms Wells pursed her lips. 'Excuse me a moment, would you?' She stalked through to the outer office and picked up the phone.

I stared at the posters on Ms Wells's wall. Anorexia, self-harm, depression. Maybe I'd become a school counsellor – it seemed like a fun job. I laughed. Probably not a good move. Ms Wells stared at me sharply as she re-entered the room, and I pulled my face back to the most serious expression I could muster.

A couple of minutes later, there was a tap on the door and Georgia came in, looking scared. When she saw me, her eyes widened and she glared.

'Sit down, Georgia.'

Georgia sat in the chair furthest from me. I pulled a face at her, but she pretended not to see me. Then there was another tap on the door and Rosie Lee let herself in. Oh, great. I sat up straight, but my heart was thumping.

'Good morning, Ms Wells,' said Rosie in her best, softest, politest voice. She must have been taking lessons from Mackenzie. Butter wouldn't melt in her mouth. 'What's going on?'

'I'm hoping you can tell me, Rosie,' said Ms Wells. 'Take a seat, would you?'

Rosie smoothed her skirt as she sat, and the second Ms Wells wasn't watching, she narrowed her eyes at me. I almost yelled out, *There! That's the look, that's what I mean!* But in a flash it was gone again. Rosie shot a glance at Georgia; Georgia stared at the carpet.

Then the door opened again, and the Head came sweeping into the room. We all scrambled to our feet.

'Sit down, everyone,' she said pleasantly, pulling back a chair for herself. 'Now, what's all this?' She smiled around the circle of chairs, then they all turned and stared at me.

Ms Wells said, 'Jessica has come to me with a most serious allegation. Jessica? Will you repeat what you told me just now?'

So I said it over again. It sounded even more lame than the first time, with Rosie Lee and Georgia and the Head and Ms Wells staring at me, all furious with me for their own reasons, but none of them noticing how furious the others were.

The Head turned to Georgia. 'Is there any truth in what Jem says?'

Points to the Head for getting my name right; points off for asking such a terrible question. Did she really expect Georgia to rat on Rosie while she was sitting right next to her?

Georgia stared at the carpet and mumbled something.

'Speak up, please, Georgia, so we can all hear.'

Georgia flung her head up; her face was scarlet. 'Rosie isn't – she doesn't – she sends me things, but—'

'You don't feel there's any malicious intent behind Rosie's actions?' suggested the Head helpfully. Georgia nodded. I closed my eyes.

The Head turned to Rosie. 'And what do you say?'

Rosie spread her hands, the picture of injured inno-cence. 'I don't know where Jem gets the idea that I'm mean to Georgia. Sure, I tease her a little, but that's what friends do.'

'I'd rather not interfere with girls' friendships,' said the Head. 'If Georgia can take a joke in the spirit in which it's intended, then I don't see the need for other people, however well-meaning, to become involved.'

Everyone stared at me.

'We've never had a bullying problem at this school,' said the Head. 'And I suspect we don't actually have one now.'

Suddenly Rosie began to cry. 'I can't believe Jem could call me a bully,' she sobbed. 'Over *nothing* — she's just jealous because I'm friends with Mackenzie and she wants to be and Georgia used to be her friend and now she's friends with me and Jem's had a falling-out with Bec Patel and Iris Kwong.' All this tumbled out in a rush.

Ms Wells ripped some tissues from the box and handed them to Georgia, who passed them to Rosie, who mopped at her eyes.

'All right, Georgia, Rosie, you can go,' said Ms Wells briskly. 'I don't think there's any need to take this any further. Jessica, would you mind staying for a moment?'

I sat down again. I heard the door click shut as Rosie and Georgia left the room. The Head leaned back in her chair and steepled her fingers and peered at me over the rim of her glasses.

'So, Jessica,' said Ms Wells. 'Rosie seemed to suggest that

you've been having a rough time in your own friendships lately. Is that the case?'

'Well, yes — I guess so — but that hasn't got anything to do with—'

'I believe in girls sorting out their own problems for themselves,' said the Head. 'I've never had much time for tattle-tales.'

'But isn't it school policy?'

The Head raised an eyebrow. 'Thank you, Jem, I don't need your help to elucidate school policy.'

Ms Wells said, 'Jessica, is there anything you'd like to talk to me about? Privately?'

'This isn't about *me*,' I said, maybe too loudly. I could feel my face getting as hot as Georgia's had been earlier. 'You're the ones who are acting like bullies!'

There was a terrible silence.

Slowly the Head rose to her feet. 'This school has always prided itself on its tradition of encouraging girls to be assertive. But I will not tolerate rudeness, aggression or disrespect. I hope I will not have to require you to suspend your studies to provide you with an opportunity to think about the difference.'

It took me a minute to untangle that, but when I did I nearly fell off my chair. The Head was threatening to *suspend* me. I stuttered, 'No, Miss Ezard. Sorry, Miss Ezard.'

'I'm extremely disappointed in you, Jessica. I'm always trying to expand the range of diversity in the backgrounds of our students. I had hoped that you would appreciate the opportunity you've been given at this school. You realise, of course, that a suspension would result in the cancellation of your scholarship.'

I couldn't speak.

'You may consider yourself on notice. Any further lapses in behaviour will result in the consequences I have outlined.'

'Yes, Miss Ezard,' I whispered. The Head swept from the room. Ms Wells put her hand on my arm. I think even she was shocked.

'It won't come to that, Jessica, I'm sure. You must know the one thing the Head can't bear is disrespectful talk.'

I knew that. I did know that. I just stood there, feeling dizzy.

'Go on.' Ms Wells gave my arm a little shake. 'You'd better get off to class. And if there's anything you want to discuss . . .'

'Thanks,' I said vaguely, and I let myself out. I couldn't even think what day it was, where I was supposed to be.

I didn't say a word to anyone, but by the end of the day it was all over the school that I'd called the Head a (insert expletive here) and I was going to be expelled.

Mum and Dad were magnificent. I didn't think they'd shout — we were not a shouty kind of family — but I was scared they'd be upset. I was more worried about them suffering than telling me off, actually. It was hard to explain the exact chain of events; I wasn't entirely sure what had happened myself. Except that I had suspension, and the threat of losing my scholarship, hanging over my head. Suspended, as it were. Ha, ha. Not that I felt like laughing.

But Dad just put his arm around me. 'Don't you worry,' he said. 'We'll sort it out. You want me to ring Miss Ezard?'

'Oh, no.' I knew that would only add fuel to the fire of the Head's wrath. 'No, I'll just keep a low profile and it'll all die down. I hope.'

'Darling,' said Mum. 'If you're not happy — if you want to look at some other schools—'

'No, no! I don't want to leave. Truly.'

'All right,' said Mum. 'If you're sure. You decide what you really want, and we'll help you make it happen.'

'Thank you,' I said, and I meant it. 'I was trying to do the right thing, you know? I was trying to help Georgia.'

'Sometimes people don't want to be helped. They have to sort it out in their own good time.' Dad hugged me. He didn't hug me much any more, since I grew up, I guess. 'And sometimes trying to do the right thing gets you a bullet in the head, eh?'

Dad always found a way to bring up Grandpa Darko in times of trouble.

I managed a small smile. 'Well, it wasn't quite that bad.'

Dad was still hugging me. 'If anyone pulls a gun on you, you let me know, and I'll come and stand in front of it. Okay?'

'Okay.'

Most of the time Dad managed to say absolutely the wrong thing, but every now and then he got it exactly right.

Next day at school was a nightmare. Literally like one of those nightmares where everyone was staring at you and you can't figure out why, and then you realise you're naked, or you can't remember how to spell *fluorescent*. (Actually maybe that's just me – but I know other people have the naked dream.)

Except I knew exactly why everyone was staring. And it wasn't because I was naked, obviously. But I felt as if I were. More than naked, I felt raw. Every glance was a needle piercing my flesh, until I was bleeding all over. It was the exact opposite of being invisible. And I didn't like it.

Everyone assumed I'd been suspended. So they were all wondering what I was doing at school. Whispering, speculating, telling each other exactly what I'd called the Head. The fact that I hadn't actually been suspended didn't seem to spoil the story.

I saw Mackenzie once, at the other end of a corridor, and I turned away. I didn't want to give her the chance to flick a wounding glance at me as well; I knew it would hurt even more coming from her.

My old gang did their best to act as human shields. Even Georgia was horrified when she found out how much trouble I was in, though she took a dim view of me trotting off to Ms Wells on her behalf, but loyalty won out and she didn't abandon me.

But, grateful as I was to them all for trying to protect me, Bec and Iris were still as irritating as ever, and what I felt about Georgia was a lot more complicated than mere irritation. If only she'd backed me up! One word from her in the counsellor's office, and none of this would have happened to me; *and* she would have got rid of Rosie.

To cap it all off, I wasn't safe, even surrounded by my human shields; the darts still found their target. The whole situation was horrible. Maybe that was why I felt a certain nostalgia for the time when I was simply, magically, gloriously friends with Mackenzie — all five minutes of it.

On Thursday, I saw Mackenzie again, coming out of the Head's office. She tossed her head back and her golden hair swung round her face. I was right over on the other side of the foyer, but her eyes locked on mine. For a long moment we stared at each other; Mackenzie's eyes seemed very bright, as if she were playing the part of the defiant princess or Maid Marian about to be sent to the dungeons. Then Frances and Phillipa swept her away, and Bec and Iris dragged me off in the opposite direction, and I couldn't see her any more.

Why had Mackenzie gone to see Miss Ezard? There were a hundred possibilities: maybe her father wanted to donate a new swimming centre, maybe the Head had asked her to give a speech before the concert, maybe Mackenzie had been granted special permission to join the Year 11s on their trip to Japan. It wasn't as if Mackenzie Woodrow was a stranger to the Head's office; she and Miss Ezard sometimes shared a joke in the corridor, they were practically buddies. There was probably a perfectly innocent explanation.

But the tilt of Mackenzie's chin and the suspicious brightness of her eyes bothered me; it chewed away at the back of my mind. Perhaps I'd been hanging round too long with Bec, but I couldn't help feeling that some skul-duggery was afoot.

On the bus the next morning, I overheard Emily Tan talking in a low, excited voice to Olivia Baxter in the seat behind me.

'Jess Casinader says Sara-Grace Fratelli says her mum's cousin — you know her mum's cousin works in the Head's office? Well, Sara-Grace says Mackenzie Woodrow *stormed* in and *demanded* to see Miss Ezard and she said if Rosie Lee was expelled, she'd leave too and take her father's funding with her, and the Head *lost* it and said how dare you try to blackmail me, and she put Mackenzie on a bond.'

'*Mackenzie*'s on a bond?' squeaked Olivia.

I couldn't believe it, either. Mackenzie Woodrow, golden girl, on a good-behaviour bond? I half-expected to see pigs flying past the bus window.

Olivia whispered, 'But what's the story with Rosie Lee?'

'Didn't you hear about that? *Apparently*, Rosie got dobbed in for bullying Georgia Harris!'

Olivia gave a strangled sound and Emily fell abruptly silent. I knew if I turned around I'd see frantic sign language and gestures in my direction. I pressed my forehead to the grimy glass of the window and prayed for my power of invisibility to return; I'd never fully appreciated the benefits of being invisible until now.

But what I mostly felt was a raging hurt. So much for Mackenzie standing up to the Nazis; she'd betrayed me. *Shouldn't you tell someone about Georgia and Rosie?* And then, when the situation heated up, she'd rushed in to save Rosie's neck. She'd got herself on a bond for worthless Rosie Lee. But no one was coming to save poor old Robin Hood from the gallows. Mackenzie had just shrugged and watched me swing.

It didn't take long for the latest developments to spread round the school. Soon everyone knew that Mackenzie had thrown herself at the Head's feet to plead for Rosie's life, and everyone knew why. Rosie Lee stalked the corridors with a triumphant swagger; I couldn't bear to even look at Mackenzie, who hid behind the curtain of her hair and pretended I didn't exist.

If it hadn't been so unfair, it would have been funny. I was threatened with suspension, and everyone treated me like a leper; Mackenzie was threatened with suspension, and she became the people's hero. Golden even in disgrace.

'You couldn't keep your mouth shut, could you?' said Georgia, with uncharacteristic bitterness. 'Now everyone thinks I'm a bully victim!'

'Because they couldn't have figured that out by *observation*?' I snapped.

Georgia's big brown eyes swam, and she fled from the room.

'I'm sorry!' I called after her.

'Don't worry, Jem. *We're* still on your side,' said Iris. She didn't need to add, *Lucky, because we're all you've got*.

'Jem, Jem, Jem,' sighed Bec, and patted my leg. Bec has always relished a catastrophe.

On Friday evening, Ms Wells rang me at home. She sounded tired. 'I've just come from a meeting with the Head,' she told me. 'She feels, on reflection, that she might have spoken in haste.'

No kidding. Of course I didn't say that.

'The Head also appreciates that you haven't made any public comments,' Ms Wells went on. Public comments? She made me sound like a world leader. 'Given your past good record, and your exemplary behaviour this week, I have a proposition to put to you. The formal warning of suspension will be lifted, on condition that you remain discreet, and your behaviour continues to be beyond reproach.'

I didn't say anything. If I remained *discreet*? It wasn't like I was going to go running to a current affairs show and complain that my school didn't take bullying seriously — then it struck me. That was exactly what they were scared of. Cautiously I said, 'And what about — the thing I told you about?'

Ms Wells sighed. 'I'll look into it. I'm going to talk to Rosie.'

'Okay.'

'So you agree?'

'You have my word,' I said, which was something I've always wanted to say. It's such a Peter Wimsey phrase. I nearly said *my word of honour*, but that might have been taking it too far.

'So you're not getting expelled?' Bec sounded almost disappointed.

'I wasn't ever going to be expelled,' I said. 'Anyway, I'm not allowed to talk about it.'

'It's a gag order,' said Iris.

'It's a *dag* order,' said Bec.

'It's a clag order — a slag order.' And Bec and Iris snorted away until I felt like banging their stupid giggling private-joking heads together.

I wouldn't want to suggest that Bec and Iris and Georgia gloated over my humiliation; they were too naturally kind, deep down, for that. But I suspected they did enjoy feeling slightly smug about the fact that I needed them, that I'd come scuttling back like an insect who'd strayed too close to a flame. They offered me shelter, and I took it, and I'd always owe them for that, and they knew it.

On the last night of the worst term of my life, with the bedroom door shut, I took the box out from under my bed and opened it. For the first time in ages I picked up the green beads. I carefully unfolded Mackenzie's poem. *Yours, always Mackenzie.* I sat there, just touching it with my finger-tips, as if Mackenzie were dead and I were a medium, trying to pick up a message from beyond. But no message came, and I packed everything up and shoved the box back under the bed.

september

The airport was pandemonium. Girls from our school, St Andrew's boys everywhere, striped blazers, shrieks of laughter. St Andrew's loved Charles Le Tan even more than our school; they were sending the whole of Year 10 *and* 11. I saw Ted, Mackenzie's boyfriend. I'd almost forgotten he existed; now I remembered in a rush that I wanted to stab him. He had a mobile phone in his hand, texting; probably texting Mackenzie goodbye. I turned my head away.

Staff from both schools raced around frantically trying to keep their groups in order and get everyone's bags checked in on time. I pitied the other passengers and the airport staff; a terror alert would almost be better than this.

The Charles Le Tan excursion was part of my probation; refusing to go would definitely have counted as reproach-worthy behaviour in the Head's eyes. So, however reluctantly, here I was. And Mackenzie's scorn had made me oddly curious. Surely the man couldn't be *that* bad?

And besides, it was exciting to be going on a trip. I hadn't been in a plane since I was ten, when we went to Croatia.

'I've never been to Sydney,' I admitted to Georgia.

Georgia's cheeks were pink with excitement. She seemed to have forgiven me for my intervention over Rosie last term; Georgia hated conflict too much to hold a grudge for long. Most importantly, though, the bullying seemed to have stopped. Unless Rosie had decided to be discreet too — though discretion wasn't exactly Rosie's style.

'Wow,' said Georgia. 'You're going to *love* it. Wait till you see the harbour, and the — Jem? What's the matter?'

I couldn't breathe; I felt the blood drain from my face. 'Nothing,' I said faintly.

I'd just seen Mackenzie pirouette up to Ted and throw her arms around him. Of course she was dragged off by a teacher almost immediately; we weren't supposed to mingle with the St Andrew's boys except under highly controlled conditions, during designated excursions. But Mackenzie wasn't even supposed to be here.

I tried to keep my voice normal. 'What's Mackenzie doing here?'

Georgia rolled her eyes. 'Didn't you hear? Apparently Mackenzie's dad's a big fan of this Le Tan guy. He met him in the States. He *loves* him. So he insisted that Mackenzie came to Sydney, and Miss Macmillan said she couldn't go to Sydney and be in the concert as well, so he said, fine, pull her out of the concert, so here she is. Jess Samuels is doing the readings instead. Miss Macmillan was *gropeable*.'

'Oh,' I said weakly. 'The universe throws us gifts.'

It was weird that the sight of Mackenzie across an airport concourse should have such an effect on me, when I saw her practically every day at school without batting an eye. It was seeing her out of context, I think; like being at Heathersett River again. She tucked her golden hair behind her ear; she smiled at Ted over her shoulder. Anyone else would have seemed cheap and flirty. But Mackenzie was . . . natural. Beautiful. Ted must have been thanking his lucky stars, to be smiled at like that, by someone like her.

I had to turn round to see him. He was watching Mackenzie, of course. He stared at her with a steady, direct gaze, very slightly smiling. Again, on someone else, it could have been a smirk, or a leer; from Ted it was like: *Here's looking at you, kid.*

Would anyone ever look at me that way? With such understanding, such adoration . . . with love? I rummaged in my bag, not for anything in particular, but because it was too painful to watch.

'You all right, Jem?'

'Just checking I've got my book.'

'The flight's only an hour,' said Georgia. 'You won't have time to read.'

'I hope I don't vomit. When we went to Croatia I was sick all the way.'

Georgia was alarmed. 'Not in front of the St Andrew's boys. That's not a good look, sticking your head in a sick-bag.'

'Thanks, Georgia.'

'Hi,' said Iris. 'Where are you guys sitting?'

We conferred over boarding passes. 'We're a couple of rows in front of you.'

'Safer at the back,' said Bec.

'So they say.'

Most of our conversations were like this now: stilted, formal. It was an impersonation of the friendship we used to have. Every day, every hollow exchange of words, was a reminder of what we'd lost.

It wasn't as if we actually disliked each other. And the pull of habit was just too strong to resist. It was too cold now, in third term, for our old corner of the quad, so we'd gravitated to a new spot near the Drama Room: neutral ground. Georgia worked hard to smooth things along, bless her. Maybe Georgia even thought we were all mates again, just like before. But Bec and Iris and I knew differently.

I'd tried to convince myself that it wasn't so bad; that I didn't feel lonely; that I didn't miss the way things used to be. Sometimes I could even kid myself that I was happy.

A knot of St Andrew's boys waited ahead of us in the queue, guffawing and shoving each other. Boys made me nervous, especially when they were in a pack. They looked nearly like men, so big in their ridiculous striped uniform, but their faces were raw and pimply under their shaggy hair, and they pushed each other and pulled faces and sniggered like preschoolers. One of them crashed into Georgia.

'Ow!'

'Shit, sorry,' he mumbled, and his mates snorted through their noses.

'Settle down, dickheads,' ordered Ted, who was wearing a shiny badge. We didn't have prefects at our school; we were all supposed to be responsible for our own behaviour. I supposed with boys they couldn't take that chance. These ones mumbled apologies and became very busy with their boarding passes.

Ted said, 'Sorry about that. Are you all right, Georgia?'

'Yeah, I think only two toes are broken.' She grinned at him shyly.

I'd forgotten that Ted and Georgia knew each other; at least I knew she knew him, but I hadn't expected that he'd know her.

Ted said to the rest of us, 'Don't pay any attention to

these idiots. The presence of so many females is making them nervous.'

I smiled before I could stop myself. It hadn't occurred to me that having girls around would make boys anxious and silly and noisy, just as having boys around was making my schoolmates shriller and gigglier than usual.

'Enjoy your trip, ladies.' Ted gave us a casual salute, and tipped an invisible hat, before he strolled away. It should have annoyed me; it could have been patronising. It was very *charming*. But somehow he did it so well that I was . . . well, charmed.

'Wow.' Iris gazed after him. 'Wouldn't he look delicious in a uniform.' He was just her type, totally Aryan.

I said, 'He is in a uniform.'

Our eyes met and for a fraction of a second we could read each other's minds, just like we used to. 'I mean a real uniform,' said Iris witheringly. 'A soldier's uniform.'

'He's very Wimsey,' I said.

'He's Mackenzie Woodrow's boyfriend,' said Georgia. 'Ted Rathbone. He's a sweetie.' She whispered in my ear, 'I'll tell you something later.'

When we were on the plane and safely buckled, she leaned close and murmured, 'Rosie and Mackenzie are sharing a room, right, and so are Ted and his friend Gus. Well, Rosie thinks they should swap rooms.'

I stared at her. 'No *way*! They'll all be expelled in two seconds if they get caught.'

Georgia shrugged. 'Ted and Gus are like Mackenzie and Rosie, you know? Ted tries to keep Gus in line, like Mackenzie does with Rosie.' She peered at me cautiously; she didn't talk to me about Rosie these days. She thought there was still a danger that I might explode unexpectedly. Seeing it was safe, she went on. 'So normally I'd say it wouldn't happen, no way. But, you know, Ted and Mackenzie are together, so maybe they won't be able to resist.'

'They'd better resist or all hell's going to break loose,' I said flatly.

'Mm,' said Georgia, and flinched as a paper pellet hit her on the ear. St Andrew's boys were flicking them up and down the plane. Even if it was only an hour, it was going to be a long flight.

I wasn't sick, luckily. And Georgia was wrong, I did have time to read. But for the last part of the flight I put my book away and gazed out at the banks of cloud that drifted past the window. Other people didn't seem as fascinated as me, but I couldn't stop staring. It was extraordinary, miraculous, to be so high, to see the parched earth spread out below and the sculptured clouds floating by. From the ground, they seemed two dimensional, painted flat onto the sky, but up here they were towering, three dimensional, magnificent.

I was still feeling dreamy when we landed, and even

through the tumult and flurry of collecting bags, having our names ticked off, lining up for buses, I felt as if part of me was still suspended in the sky, detached from everything. It was amazing enough to see the earth from the height of an aeroplane. What must it be like to see it from space, a perfect marble, so separate, so self-contained?

Hadn't I had a discussion about this once before . . .?

That night on Mt Emmaline with Mackenzie. Of course. *Stupid* that after all these months that memory was still painful. I didn't want to think about Mackenzie.

So I heaved my bag on my back and queued for the bus with everyone else, and forced my mind elsewhere.

The hotel we were booked into was nothing flash, but it was clean, and hey, it was a hotel. Lord Peter Wimsey was hardly ever out of hotels, but I didn't stay in them with the same regularity; this was an adventure. Jessica Samuels and Rosie Lee complained that it was a dump, but it was thrilling for me. It was exciting to claim a bed, and figure out how the TV worked, and exclaim over the little bottles in the bathroom (the little bottles in the mini-bar had been removed), and throw open the curtains and crane for a view. Okay, there wasn't anything to see, but the square grey office building opposite was a *Sydney* office building. We were in Sydney, and somewhere out there was the harbour, and the bridge, and the Opera House, and the Mardi Gras, and the Blue Mountains . . .

'The Mardi Gras is in summer, isn't it?' said Georgia.

'It's still Sin City. Corruption and hedonism on every corner, waiting to seduce us . . .'

'We're more likely to get seduced inside the hotel,' said Georgia. 'With all these boys around.'

Even though the St Andrew's boys were on a different floor, we could sense their presence: muffled feet like distant thunder overhead, croaky voices, far off howls and shouts and thumps. And when we went down to the restaurant for lunch, there was a faint sweaty odour in the lift.

Lunch was not exciting. On the other side of the restaurant, Mackenzie pulled a face as she forked through what was allegedly a beef salad, but tasted more like boiled shoe.

'The lettuce is *slimy*.' Bec shuddered; she hated all forms of slime.

'Good practice for Oxford.' Iris chewed stoically. 'The food there will be inedible.'

'Good practice for this afternoon,' I said. 'Charles Le Tan will probably be pretty slimy, too.'

'Careful,' said Bec. 'Was that a public comment?'

I said nothing.

'Cheesecake!' Georgia nodded to the dessert table, where the boys of St Andrew's were clustering like flies on a carcass.

'Hardly any of the girls are going up,' I said.

'They don't want the boys to think they're pigs,' said Georgia.

'That's ridiculous,' I said, and I marched up to the table and loaded a plate. Iris and Bec weren't far behind; Georgia hesitated, but finally she came too. The desserts were beautiful. Jess Casinader and Sara-Grace Fratelli cast wistful eyes at our plates, laden with chocolate mousse and raspberry pavlova and some kind of hazelnut cream meringue thing, and I was intensely grateful that I wasn't the kind of girl who cared what boys thought of her appetite. Rosie Lee didn't care either, it seemed; her plate was piled nearly as high as Bec's.

The irony was that none of the boys were paying attention to the girls anyway; they were too busy stuffing their own faces.

Soon it was time for the staff to herd us back on our buses to go and hear Charles Le Tan. They looked exhausted already; we could tell they were glad this excursion only lasted till Sunday afternoon.

The stadium was massive. It was one of the venues for the Olympics, and I remembered seeing it on TV as a kid, filled to the brim with cheering, roaring spectators. It was nearly filled to the brim now. Apparently not everyone in the world shared Mackenzie Woodrow's disdain for the Inspiration Guy; in fact, it seemed there were thousands of people willing to pay a hefty sum to hear his words of so-called wisdom.

The fact that Mackenzie's dad was such a big fan prejudiced me against him, I must admit. I don't think

Mackenzie's dad and Robin Hood Jem, champion of the powerless, would agree on much, actually.

That was a joke. Kind of. I'd tried being a rebel and look where it got me! My rebellious days were over. Blink and you'd have missed it.

We all filed into the stadium murmuring and shuffling our feet, unsure whether we should behave as if we were in a cathedral or at a football match. Just the fact that there was such a huge crowd gave the stadium an amazing atmosphere, and all the other people were buzzing, yet reverent, too. It was a solemn thing to pay that much money to hear one man speak; there was anticipation in the air. As well as the lingering odour of the St Andrew's boys.

At one point I thought I felt someone staring at me, and I swung around, but no one was there. Well, several thousand people were there, obviously, but none of them were looking at me. I glimpsed Ted Rathbone a few rows back, but he was gazing off to the left, toward Mackenzie. We'd all been told to switch off our mobiles; a lot of people hadn't, but the golden twins had been obedient, so they were signalling to each other, nodding and smiling and gesticulating with their hands. Like the mating ritual of a pair of exotic birds. I swung round in my seat again.

Georgia stiffened beside me and stood abruptly. 'I have to go to the toilet.'

'*Again?* You just went!' I squeezed back to let her past, then it occurred to me that I should probably go myself before the show started, so I hurried after her down the steps and out into the echoing concrete concourse. 'Georgia, wait!'

She didn't hear; she disappeared into the nearest ladies loo and I followed.

It was surprisingly empty; everyone else must have finished their last-minute rush already. Georgia and I were cutting it fine; I could hear a voice rolling through the stadium, Charles Le Tan's warm-up guy. A couple of doors were closed; one of them must have been Georgia.

I hurried into a cubicle and did what I had to do, but when I came out there was no sign of Georgia. I washed my hands. From the stadium came a muffled roar of laughter and the amplified chuckle of the warm-up guy. Then I heard another sound: the noise of someone throwing up.

'Georgia! Are you okay?'

Georgia shot out of a cubicle like a rocket. 'I'm fine.' She glanced nervously behind her.

The retching noise was repeated, then a muffled voice from inside the closed cubicle said, 'Piss off, Martinic.'

'It's Rosie,' hissed Georgia unnecessarily.

'Is she okay?' I whispered back.

The toilet flushed, the door banged open and Rosie Lee appeared, wiping her mouth on some toilet paper. 'I'm fine,' she said. She threw the wad of paper into the toilet and fished in her pocket. 'Mint?'

I was nonplussed. Rosie seemed very cool and collected for someone who'd just been chucking her guts up. 'Do you want a drink of water? Fresh air?'

Rosie tossed back a couple of mints and clicked the packet shut. 'How about you mind your own business, Jem? Though that's not something you're very skilled at, is it?'

I said to Georgia, 'What's going on?'

Georgia's eyes flickered to Rosie. 'Um — too much cake?'

'Tell your friend to get lost, Georgie,' drawled Rosie.

The possibilities whirled through my mind. Pregnancy? Some mysterious illness? Drugs? Then at last I got it. 'Bulimia,' I said under my breath. 'Great. Like you haven't got enough problems.'

Rosie's eyes narrowed. 'Aren't you clever. But you're the one who's got problems, Martinic.'

'Rosie . . .' Georgia faltered. 'Maybe we should go outside . . .'

Rosie ignored her. She stepped towards me. 'You want to know the real reason you nearly got expelled? You want to know what Mackenzie's been saying about you?'

My mouth was dry. I couldn't speak. From far, far away, there came a roar of applause and stamping feet and the voice of the warm-up guy reached a crescendo: *Cha-arles — Le — TAN!*

Rosie stood close to me. 'Mackenzie told everybody you're a lesbian. She said you were making moves on her at camp. She said you couldn't wait to get into her pants. Everyone knows: the staff, the Head, everyone. That's why she had to stop hanging out with you. She just wanted to be friends, but you wanted more.'

I opened my mouth. I looked at Georgia. She said faintly, 'There is a — a rumour. There's graffiti in the second floor toilets.'

I felt sick.

'Mackenzie went to the Head, after you tried to get me thrown out for bullying — remember that?' Rosie sneered. 'Mackenzie told her not to believe a word you said, because you're just a frustrated dyke. That's why you're on a bond. The Head doesn't want you at the school. Bad influence, get the school a bad reputation. She thinks you've got no self-control. If you weren't such a brain, you'd already be gone.' Rosie snapped her fingers and I jumped. 'What do you think of that then, Miss Clever Jem?'

I found a croaky voice at the very bottom of my throat. 'It's not true. No one thinks — and they wouldn't care—'

'Hah!' said Rosie. 'So you admit it.'

I turned back to Georgia, but her eyes slid away. She bit her bottom lip.

I forced myself to sound calm. 'Mackenzie wouldn't say that.'

'Wanna bet?' said Rosie. She tilted her head and blew me three hard, contemptuous kisses. She and Georgia watched as I turned away.

Very slowly I dragged myself back along the curving, empty concourse. The sound of my footsteps was drowned by the roar from the stadium. I climbed the concrete steps, each foot like lead. The crowd in the stadium was hushed, and on the brightly lit stage a man strode up and down, as small as an insect. I could have squashed him with my thumb. His huge voice reverberated through the arena. The sound washed through me, lifted me and carried me away.

I was drifting in space; the earth was very far away. I stared at the stage, but I saw nothing; I heard the huge voice echo and thrum, but the words were just noise, the static hiss of background radiation. I drifted, spinning in slow motion, in the cold, cold vastness of the universe.

Everything was coming apart. Every particle, every fragment of existence, drifting and expanding, further and further, until nothing touched, every last contact severed. I was all alone, and it was very cold out there.

The voice of the inspiration guy fell from a shout to a low, clear murmur, and suddenly it was as if he were speaking just to me, in that whole crowded stadium, as if he were reaching out and touching me.

He said, 'You decide who you truly are. *You* decide. Not

me, not your family, not your friends, not your spouse. Every day, every minute, you are becoming the person you choose to be. This is what you have to ask yourself: *Is this who I choose to be?*'

Then his voice raised again and he turned away and he was shouting something about making a difference, and choices, and being positive, but for me it was as if time stood still. I sat there in a daze for an hour and a half. I stood up when everyone else did, I sat when they sat. I shouted when other people shouted, I was quiet when they were quiet. But I didn't hear another word.

I thought about all the choices I'd made, all the actions that made me who I was. I thought about Bec and Iris, and the way I'd hidden beside them, invisible and safe, for so long. I thought about saying yes to Richard Patel, and saying no. I thought about Heathersett River and the touchy-feely night, and the night Mackenzie and I held hands and sang to the stars. I thought about trying to help Georgia and how it had all gone so horribly wrong. I thought about calling the Head a bully. I thought about Grandpa Darko and the Nazis.

And I thought about Mackenzie. I stared at the back of her golden head and I remembered every conversation we'd ever had, every look, every gesture. It was like peeling off skin, digging at my flesh; it hurt so much, and I knew I shouldn't do it, but once I started, I couldn't stop. And I knew that whatever Mackenzie did, whatever she said, however she'd betrayed me, I had to believe that the brief window of our friendship was precious, even if it was gone, even if it was destroyed forever; I had to believe it was real, because I had made it, I had chosen it, just as much as she had. It wasn't a gift she'd bestowed on me: it was both of us, holding up our cupped hands together to the stars.

When at last the lights went up I felt weird and shaky as if I'd run a marathon. I was exhausted, from thinking and from the effort of trying not to cry. But then I saw that heaps of people had been crying − grown women, with smudged mascara, even grown men looking suspiciously red round the eyes. People held each other's arms for support, dazed, as they tottered out onto the concourse.

I craned around for Georgia, but she hadn't come back to her seat. Then I saw Mackenzie; she was scanning the crowd, searching for Ted I guess, or Rosie, and when she saw me our eyes met and locked for a second. I don't know what kind of expression came over my face, but I saw her face change before I turned away. I couldn't look at her for long. It was the difference between picking at a scab and jabbing a knife into your arm.

I shoved my way past the shuffling, muttering crowd toward the exit. The noise, the heat, the press of the crowd, were all making me feel faint. I even started to panic, like on my first day of school, that I wouldn't find the bus, that I'd be trapped here and never get home.

'Jem! Jem, wait!'

It was Bec and Iris, running up behind me. We were outside the arena now, pushing against the crowd around the perimeter toward the buses.

'Jem! What did you think?'

'Yeah, it was – Have you seen Georgia?'

'No.' Iris grabbed my arm; her face was glowing. 'Jem, listen, I've got something to say to you.'

'Me too,' chimed in Bec. 'But Iris wants to go first.'

I stopped. They looked – odd. *Radiant*. I don't think I'd ever seen Bec or Iris radiant before. 'Okay, what?'

Iris said, 'Charles Le Tan – he's right. You know that thing he said? It's absolutely true. What will it matter in fifty years? What *will* it matter?'

'Um . . .' I hadn't heard him say that, so I didn't feel qualified to comment.

'That wasn't the important thing!' Bec said. 'The important thing was about negativity, how it holds you back, distorts your life. That was the main thing. Don't you think?'

'Well . . .' I said slowly. They seemed to have heard a different speech from the one I'd heard; possibly two different speeches. Maybe Charles Le Tan was like the Magic Pudding, and everyone came away with a different taste, different words of wisdom. Besides, I wasn't so sure that a little negativity was such a bad thing. A nip of sarcasm, a sprinkle of scepticism, that was what made Bec and Iris who they were. That was why . . . I realised it with a jolt. They were better friends with each other than they were with me because they suited each other better; they were a better fit. It had just taken us four years to work it out. And we could all still be friends; just not best friends. And that was okay.

'Anyway,' said Iris. 'I've decided to forgive you.'

'Me too,' said Bec. They beamed at me as if we'd all just won the lottery.

I *literally* did not know what to say. They forgave me? Who decided I was the one who had to be forgiven?

But then — they both looked so pleased. So excited at the idea of being proper friends again. If I said something cutting now, if I walked away, that would be the end. Did I really want to lose Bec and Iris forever, my second-best friends, over some paltry pointless quarrel?

It flashed through my mind that the really honourable, gracious, noble, superior, Wimsey thing to do would be to accept their forgiveness, to forgive *them*, without even telling them. Let them think they were forgiving me; they'd feel good. And the truth was, I didn't actually care that much about the rights and wrongs of it all. The choice was up to me.

'Okay,' I said at last. 'I accept your forgiveness.'

Bec's smile wobbled, as if she wasn't quite sure whether I was taking the mickey (maybe I was, just a smidge). But Iris's grin grew wider, if possible.

Far away in the distance, beside the bus, Ms Wells was shouting.

'Quick,' said Bec. 'We have to hurry. Like Charles Le Tan said, time's running out.'

'Did he say that?' said Iris. 'He didn't say that.'

I said, 'Come on.'

And we all linked arms, just like we would have done when we were in Year 7, and we marched, the three of us, side by side, through the crowd.

september

'What happened to you? Where have you *been*?' I sat up on the bed and closed my book as Georgia slipped into our hotel room.

'Chill out, it's okay.' She plumped down on the other bed. 'We were on the other bus, that's all.'

'We? You and Rosie Lee?'

'Of course me and Rosie.' She jumped up again and circled the room, picking things up at random and putting them down.

'Does anyone else know about Rosie?'

'About—?' Georgia mimed sticking her finger in her throat. 'I dunno, I don't think so.' A shy, almost proud expression came over her face. 'I think she's only told me. I know she hasn't told Mackenzie.'

'So it's your secret?'

'Yeah.'

I was silent. That was a pretty big secret. I could almost understand how the privilege of holding a secret like that, being the trusted one, the only, could seem like the most important thing in the world. Mackenzie admitting she wanted to be a cook was nothing compared to that.

I pushed the memory away. That was irrelevant now. Since then, Mackenzie had invented a secret that didn't exist, and spread it round the whole school. When I thought about that, my throat felt like it was closing up.

I forced myself to focus on the matter at hand. 'So she's not getting any help? She hasn't told Ms Wells?'

Georgia shook her head. 'She thinks Ms Wells is an idiot . . .' Suddenly she looked alarmed. 'Jem, *you* won't tell Ms Wells, will you?'

'Do you think I would, after last time?'

There was a silence in the room.

'I guess not,' said Georgia awkwardly.

'But someone should tell someone.' I shifted on the bed. 'Georgia, if no one else knows . . .' Rosie told me today, she didn't have to. Maybe she *wants* us to tell, to try and get help – maybe she can't do it herself . . . And she knows I'm the kind of interfering, do-gooding, know-all type who *would* run and dob.'

Georgia was horrified. 'Oh, no, Jem, you can't. You can't do that. Rosie would never forgive me.'

I flopped backward. 'All right, I give up. Let's just sit around and watch Rosie vomit herself to death. I don't give a fig what happens to her.'

And it was true, on one level I didn't care what happened to Rosie. She was a first-class, prize-winning, show-stopping viper-cow. But I also knew I wouldn't be able to let it go that easily; it was going to nag at me till I did something. And I wonder, now, if Rosie knew that too. Whether I liked it or not, I seemed to have turned into the kind of person who did things.

Georgia sat down on the end of my bed. 'Jem. I need to ask you a favour. You know how Rosie wanted to swap rooms? Well, Ted disagreed, but he suggested they have a party in his and Gus's room instead.'

'What a great idea. So twenty people can get into trouble instead of four.'

'There'll only be trouble if we don't come . . .'

'If *we* don't come?'

'Rosie wants me to go and I want you to come with me.'

'No way.'

'Jem, you have to. I'm begging you.' Tears swam in Georgia's eyes. 'I'm worried about Rosie, I don't want her to go by herself. And she will go. Anything could happen. Those boys – the more of us there are, the safer it'll be.'

'Give me one good reason why I shouldn't tell Ms Wells.'

'Gus is on a warning and if he gets into trouble again he'll be expelled.'

'Good. Problem solved.' I picked up my book.

'He hasn't done anything . . . one of the teachers has a grudge against him . . .'

'Oh, please. I'm telling Ms Wells right now.' I put down my book.

'You can't, Jem, Rosie'll blame me and she'll never speak to me again.'

'Good thing number two.'

'Jem!' wailed Georgia. '*Please!*' Her face crumpled.

I knew the sensible thing to do, the proper thing, would be to run to Ms Wells and report the lot of them, right?

But instead I said, '*Okay*, I'll come.'

Dumb decision. Dumb, and wrong, and I can't justify it, except that Georgia was so forlorn, so desperate, and — she's my friend, and I wanted to help her. Maybe I did feel, deep down, that I owed her one after the last fiasco, getting her branded a bully victim by the whole school. And I didn't want anything bad to happen her; not even to Rosie, really.

And I didn't want to be a dobber, again.

And maybe, at the very cobwebby back of my mind, there was half a thought that if I went to a party with boys, then people wouldn't think I was a dyke . . . I might even meet a charming boy . . .

And there was the adrenaline afterglow of the inspiration guy, which had made me feel a little reckless and brave and in control of my life, and ready for an adventure. Hah.

The 'party' started at ten o'clock. The staff were patrolling the corridors every half hour; they weren't stupid. But Georgia and I got past them, and so did half of St Andrew's, apparently, because the room was crowded. Very crowded.

When Georgia and I arrived, every head swivelled in our direction and silence fell. It was excruciating. I shrank behind Georgia, and of course it was her they were staring at, really; I was just getting the overflow. But I knew how an alien would feel if it did land on our planet. It was as if these boys had never seen a girl before.

'Come in, ladies,' said a boy with curly hair.

Georgia said, 'Hi, Gus.'

There were boys on the beds, boys on the chairs, boys on the floor. It was stuffy, and though everyone was obviously trying hard to stay quiet, there was a constant rumble of noise, occasionally broken by an exploding snigger. The lights were low, but it was impossible to miss the gleam of bottles being passed from hand to hand.

'Make room for the ladies!' said Gus, and three boys shifted hastily off the nearest bed so we could sit down.

With so many boys packed into the room, I was almost certain that someone could see up my skirt and down my top and any other angle you could think of.

A boy leaning against the wall by the bed held out a bottle. 'Beer?'

'No thanks.'

'At least offer her a fresh one, Royston,' came a voice from across the room, and Ted Rathbone emerged from the bathroom with two stubbies. Out of uniform he was only slightly less handsome; instead of being slicked back, his fair hair flopped casually over his forehead. He waded through the sprawled bodies to hand the beers to me and Georgia.

I was so nervous I actually took a swig before I realised what I was doing. Great. Now when we got caught I couldn't even say I hadn't been drinking. The beer was bitter; I decided not to have any more. But I nursed the stubby, just to do something with my hands; and if I didn't hold it, someone else would only drink it, right?

'Great party,' I murmured to Georgia. 'This is really worth getting expelled for.'

Whispered conversations had started up again, but eyes still swivelled in our direction. No one spoke to us. I caught Ted watching us and I gave him an uncertain smile. He didn't smile back, but he looked at me gravely and took another mouthful of beer. I was disappointed he was drinking; I'd decided that he was going to be the sober, responsible member of this gathering, that at some point he'd shepherd everyone off to bed before anything bad happened. But apparently not.

Then it hit me. Mackenzie would be at this party.

I stood up abruptly.

'Where are you going?' hissed Georgia.

'Back to our room. This is stupid.'

'Stay — you can't leave me here on my own!'

'Then come with me.'

'But Rosie . . .'

'Rosie isn't even here!'

Right on cue, there was a tap at the door and Rosie and Mackenzie walked in. A sigh of satisfaction ran through the room and every boy sat up straight. They'd stared at me and Georgia all right, but at the sight of those two golden girls, they positively salivated. I took another bitter swig.

Rosie wrapped her arms round Gus and stuck her tongue down his throat. Nice. Some of the boys sniggered, some made encouraging guttural noises, but others were embarrassed as I was.

Ted stepped across the bodies to reach Mackenzie and they kissed too — a polite, barely lingering meeting of lips — but for some reason that was just as hard to watch as Rosie and Gus. And okay, I admit it, underneath the embarrassment was a great fat slab of envy. Would anyone ever want to kiss me like that?

Apart from Richard Patel. Who didn't count.

What if my first kiss turned out to be my last? What a depressing thought. I had another mouthful of beer. Didn't taste so bitter now, it went down quite smoothly, in fact.

Then Rosie turned to Georgia and threw her arms around *her*. 'You came!' She almost fell onto the bed and burst into giggles; she seemed pretty unsteady already.

Someone hissed, 'Sssh!' and Rosie stifled her laughter. I shifted over to give her room, which wedged me up against the bedhead. The mood in the room had lifted; suddenly everyone was animated, smiling, on show. It was as if they'd all been waiting for the audience, and at last the performance could begin.

I guess I could have left then. Rosie certainly wasn't on her own now. Gus sat down and before long his hands were all over her. She paid no attention, or pretended to pay no attention; she was deep in conversation with Georgia, who also pretended to pay no attention, and after a few minutes some other boys joined the circle and soon they were chatting and laughing away.

Mackenzie and Ted stood quietly on the far side of the room, arms round each other's waists, like parents survey-ing their kid's party. They looked so steady, so right together, that my heart lurched and I lowered my eyes.

I should have left. But I pulled my legs up onto the bed and took another sip of beer and watched the room.

No one talked to me. It sounds mad, but I was almost happy scrunched up on that bed. I was invisible, just the way I liked it. Time passed. People talked, and brought out more beer, and giggled. Some boys left; more space opened up. Rosie lay sprawled on the bed, her feet almost touching my head, but it was like we were in parallel dimensions, a force field between us. Georgia had slipped onto the floor, talking earnestly to two boys about vet courses. A group of boys sat on the carpet between the beds, discussing football, and every so often one of them would fling out an arm and whack my leg and glance over his shoulder and say, oh, sorry, and I'd smile distantly and shift my leg aside. Somewhere behind me Mackenzie and Ted talked and smiled, holding court, paying no attention to me. The room seemed far away; voices blurred and echoed. This was okay, this was relaxed, no problem. A new cold beer appeared beside me and I drank some; then I needed to go to the toilet and somehow I unfolded myself and picked my way across the room, which tilted under my feet until I reached the bathroom.

It was very bright in there. I studied myself in the mirror. Was I drunk? I considered my reflection at some length and decided that I wasn't. I drank some water and splashed my face and felt better.

When I came out, Rosie and Gus had moved and my little spot at the top of the bed had gone. In fact everyone had shifted around; more boys had left and the rest had congealed into one group. Music played softly and the mood had altered again. Rosie sat up and laughed; Gus tilted a beer and ran his hand up her thigh.

I tried to squeeze beside Georgia. 'We should go.'

'Oh – not yet.'

'It's late, come on.'

She squinted at her watch. 'Wait a few minutes, it's nearly one o'clock, Ms Wells'll catch us.'

'She won't be on patrol now.'

'Just a few more minutes,' pleaded Georgia.

'Okay, five more minutes.'

There wasn't room for me to sit beside her so I had to perch on the other bed, not far from Mackenzie. I wasn't having fun any more; I was twitchy and anxious. We'd been so lucky to get away with this, all I wanted now was to be safe in bed and asleep.

Then I heard Gus's voice, a little louder than before. 'Go on, do it. Go on.'

A shiver ran through the room, an intake of breath, and then a wordless rumble, an urging. I didn't understand what was happening. I inched back toward the safety of the wall, flinching from that intense, greedy noise.

Rosie tossed back her hair and laughed. She raised her eyebrows at Georgia, who laughed too, but uncertainly. Then they leaned together across the bed and kissed. As their mouths opened wider, the boys' low chorus grew louder, more excited, and Rosie and Georgia drew out their kiss, playing their audience, feeling their own power, and when they broke apart they both looked around the room, laughing and triumphant.

I felt sick. I couldn't believe Georgia would do something so cheap. And now the boys were worked up, what next? Would she take her clothes off? Couldn't she see that the boys were the ones with the real power here, not her?

But now Gus had swivelled around and was leering at the other side of the room. My side of the room. Leering at me, at me and Mackenzie.

'Your turn, girls.'

Ted said calmly, 'Rack off, Gus, you're drunk.'

'And you're not? Come on, Mackenzie, don't wuss out, you're not frigid, are you? Ted says you're not. Come on, it's your turn, you and your friend.'

An unpleasant, rhythmic murmur rippled round the room, and hardened. Most of the boys were grinning, but for the first time I felt frightened. I couldn't reach the door without going past them; they could grab me without even needing to stand up.

Instinctively I turned to Mackenzie, and found she'd inched closer to me across the bed; we were almost huddled together. And then, at last, anger welled up inside me. How dare they force us into this! I glared at Gus. 'Piss off!'

The boys gave a low, threatening growl, and a shiver of movement passed through the room as they edged closer to the bed, closing the trap.

Mackenzie's fingers tightened on my arm. 'Don't, Jem.'

I heard Georgia's voice, high and frightened. 'Better do what they want . . .'

Mackenzie and I looked at each other. Her hand was still on my arm and I felt her grip me tighter and tighter as her face moved closer to mine. Her breath was hot against my cheek. I was breathing fast.

Suddenly Mackenzie cried out and flung my arm away. She covered her face with her hands, and stumbled to the door.

'Mackenzie!' said Ted in a hoarse whisper, and he was on his feet too, and I staggered up and floundered after them both, dizzily tripping over boys' legs, and pleased, with one corner of my mind, that I managed to kick some of them. I grabbed the door just as it closed behind Ted. As I stumbled into the corridor, I saw him disappear through the fire door. I sprinted after him, flung the door open, but then the beer hit me and I gasped for breath as I staggered up the stairs, clutching the rail. I could hear their feet clattering on the steps above me, and I heard Ted call Mackenzie's name, and the heavy door to the roof swung open and slammed shut.

I dragged myself up the steps, head spinning, heart pounding. Finally I burst out into the cool, crisp night and felt the fresh air drench my burning face; I stood there for a minute just gulping it in. My head cleared. Then I heard voices. They were speaking quietly, but I heard every word.

Ted said, 'You didn't have to do it if you didn't want to. It doesn't do anything for me . . .'

Mackenzie laughed, a wobbly, strained laugh that I'd never heard before. 'But I did want to,' she almost sobbed. 'I did want to. That's the trouble.'

'I know,' came Ted's voice, and it was muffled, as if he was hugging her. 'I know, mate, I know.'

Mackenzie murmured into his chest, and I knew I should leave, that I shouldn't be listening to this, but just then the heavy fire door clicked shut behind me like a gunshot, and Ted said sharply, 'What was that? Who's there?'

I stepped out into the half-light cast from the higher office buildings and the three of us stood blinking at each other. 'It's only me.'

Mackenzie sobbed out, 'Jem — *oh*!' as if she were choking, and she broke away from Ted and fled for the cover of an air-conditioning tower.

'Mackenzie!' I tried to follow her, but Ted grabbed me.

'Give her a minute,' he said, kindly, but firmly, and he sat us down on the edge of a concrete block with his arm around my shoulder. Side by side, we stared out at the city lights.

Ted said, 'I'm sorry about all that. Gus is — Gus is a dickhead.'

'It's not your fault.'

'Yeah, it is. I let them go too far.'

'You couldn't stop them.'

'Yeah, I could.'

We sat in silence for a minute then Ted said, 'You know it's you she really cares about, don't you.'

I shook my head. 'Yeah, right. We were supposed to be friends, then she—'

'Jem, I know everything, believe me.' Ted laughed ruefully. 'Sounds as if I know more about it than you do.'

I stiffened. 'What's that supposed to mean?'

'Hey, settle down.' He squeezed me round the shoulders till I relaxed. 'Better let Mackenzie do the talking.'

'She doesn't talk to me anymore.' To my shame, tears prickled behind my eyelids.

'She will.' Ted pulled back and I tried to focus on his face in the dim light. 'You don't get it, do you. Listen: it's *you* she cares about. Do you understand?'

I was silent for a moment. At last I said, 'No. Yes. No. But – what about you? Aren't you—?'

'Don't worry about me,' said Ted. 'I'm okay. But I'd better go and clean up that mess downstairs before we all get chucked out of the hotel and then out of our schools.' He stood up and I saw the shadowy mass of Mackenzie outlined against the sky.

'All right, mate?' Ted asked.

'Yeah.' Mackenzie let out a shuddering breath.

'Sure?'

'I – I think so.'

They hugged, a quick firm hug, and Ted gave her a brotherly pat on the back. And then Ted was gone.

Mackenzie sat beside me, leaving a gap between us. 'So,' she said. 'Here we are.'

I said, 'Ted's lovely.'

'Yeah. He is, he really is. We just clicked, you know, I think we'll be friends forever.'

'Friends forever, eh.' I could hear the hard edge to my own voice.

The faint hum of traffic drifted up to us from the street below. My breath was shallow and my heart was thumping, as if I were scared of what was going to happen next. And I was scared. But at the same time suddenly I knew I wanted it, I was dizzy with wanting it.

'Here's the thing,' whispered Mackenzie. 'I did want to kiss you. I've wanted to kiss you ever since that night under the stars.'

My heart beat very fast. It was a surreal moment. The world seemed to tip upside down, as if the city lights had swung overhead to become a universe of stars. There was a pause that seemed very long, but probably only lasted a few seconds, before I remembered that Mackenzie was waiting for me to reply. I swallowed. 'I — I don't know what to say.'

'What I'd *like* you to say is, that's great, Mackenzie. I feel the same way.' She gave me a tight, unnatural smile, and with a shock I realised that she was terrified.

Instinctively I laid my hand on her arm. 'I do . . .'

'You *do*?' Amazement and relief broke over her face. 'You do?'

I'd never had such power over another person before. It was like playing with explosives: one wrong move and I might blow us both to smithereens.

'I do,' I said softly. 'But . . .'

Her face fell. That was one thing about Mackenzie, you always knew exactly what she was feeling. No, that's not true. In fact, most of the time, I was starting to realise, she wore a mask that showed the same emotions as everyone else, the expected emotions. She was always acting.

But now she was letting me see the true Mackenzie underneath, raw and vulnerable and absolutely real. She was letting me see everything, trusting me with the biggest secret of all. It took my breath away.

In a small voice she said, 'But?'

'Hang on . . . let me get this straight . . .'

'Not the best choice of words, Jem.'

'I guess not.'

We were quiet for a minute. 'So have you wanted to kiss – any other girls? *Have* you actually—'

'No – I mean, yeah. No. No one else.' She let out a deep sigh. 'But I always had an idea, at the back of my mind.'

'Wow,' I said uncertainly. Then I remembered, and my voice hardened. 'But why did you tell everyone that *I* was a dyke, that I made moves on you?'

'*What?* I never said that! Why would you think that?'

'Attack is the best defence? I don't know. Rosie Lee said—'

'Oh, *Rosie!* Well, that explains it.' Mackenzie pushed back her hair. 'Use your head, Jem, you're supposed to be so smart. Rosie's been jealous of you since the day we met. Since the day we became friends, anyway. She was always my best friend, since primary school, and suddenly *you* come along and you're all I can talk about, all I think about, the only person I want to spend time with – of course she was jealous.'

My face was burning. *All I think about, all I can talk about.* I couldn't take it in, that Mackenzie felt that way about me.

I said, 'Rosie's got bulimia.'

'*What?* Really? Are you sure?' Mackenzie stared at me, then closed her eyes. She took a deep breath before she opened them again. 'Bulimia. Oh, God! I've really dropped the ball with Rosie. I haven't been a very good friend to her this year. Too – preoccupied. Oh, Rosie.'

'She needs help. Georgia's trying, but she can't do it on her own.'

'Yeah.' Mackenzie rubbed her face with her hands. 'Okay. Will you – will you help me? Though I'd understand if you didn't want to,' she added quickly.

'I don't know how much Rosie wants my help, to tell you the truth. She's giving a pretty good impression of hating my guts.'

'She doesn't hate you. She's just insecure.'

'Hmm.' I wasn't so sure.

'Anyway, I don't want to talk about Rosie now.'

'No, me either.'

Talking about Rosie's insecurity reminded me of how I'd felt when I'd discovered Mackenzie had a boyfriend. I said abruptly, 'What about Ted? You guys seem so – so perfect together.'

'Oh, I love Ted, I do. But not like *that*. And he knows, he knows how I feel. About – you.' Her hair swung forward as she bent her head, hiding her face. I was glad of that; I wasn't sure I could have had this conversation except in the dark.

I fixed my eyes straight ahead at the city lights that sparkled to the horizon, and heard my stiff little voice say, 'Did you kiss him?'

Mackenzie laughed wearily. 'Oh, yeah. What, did you think we just held hands? Yeah, and it was nice. But it wasn't . . .' Her voice trailed away, then she said, 'I want to be normal, Jem. I want to be like everyone else. I don't want to be an old butch dyke with a shaved head and overalls . . .'

I couldn't help laughing. 'You have to meet my mum's friend Anna. She's the most elegant, cool, amazing person. She's not like that *at all*.'

'Really?' Mackenzie sounded doubtful. Then she sighed. 'God, if my dad finds out, he'll freak. That was why – I shut you out. I realised that I – realised how I felt about you, and

I was scared. I was so scared of being — like that. And scared that you'd tell me to get lost. I dropped all those hints, but you never seemed to catch any of them. So I guessed you didn't feel the same . . .'

'I just never even thought about it,' I said honestly. 'It never occurred to me.'

Her voice shrank to a whisper. 'I couldn't even talk to you. And I'm so sorry, Jem. I'm so sorry.'

There was a lump in my throat. I tried to swallow it.

'Mackenzie, if you didn't tell Miss Ezard I was — if you didn't tell her I'd, you know, gone after you . . . You did speak to her, though, didn't you? About Rosie? I heard you threatened to leave if Rosie got expelled.'

'If *Rosie*—?' Mackenzie half-gasped, half-laughed. 'I said I'd walk out if *you* got expelled.'

'*What*?' I clutched at the concrete block we were sitting on while the world rearranged itself again. So Maid Marian had tried to rescue Robin Hood after all . . . 'But the story was—'

Mackenzie waved her hand impatiently. 'Maybe someone heard me say *my friend* and assumed it was Rosie, who knows. God, no wonder you wouldn't talk to me, if you thought I'd done that after I *made* you go to Ms Wells. Not that it did any good. Just got us both on bonds.'

'Well, we're still here.'

'Yeah.' She kicked her heel against the concrete.

'I can't believe you did that, for me. That was so brave.'

'Nah, that was nothing. It was the only thing I could think of. Anyway, it's true, I didn't want to stay at school if you weren't there, I couldn't *stand* it.'

There was a pause while Mackenzie's words disappeared into the cool night air.

Then I said quietly, 'Mackenzie, I just don't know if – if this is me. I never thought about it before.'

Mackenzie turned her head away, and her voice was flat. 'So you are telling me to get lost.'

'No! No, I'm not . . . I just need some time. I need to think about it.'

She turned back to face me. 'Just tell me, Jem, I can take it. I've imagined this so many times. Sometimes you tell me to back off, but then sometimes you lean over and . . . kiss me . . .'

There was an electric silence.

'If I *do* kiss you,' I said firmly. 'It won't be because a room full of boys are getting off on it.'

Mackenzie laughed, her own proper happy laugh.

I said, 'You're Mackenzie Woodrow, you've got everything. Why would you even look at me?'

'Are you kidding? You're smart, and funny . . . I don't know, just – your hands, the shape of your hands – the way you always walk so fast, like you've got somewhere important to go. Your hair, how it springs straight back out when you tuck it behind your ears.' Her voice dropped to a whisper. 'Your mouth.'

I felt myself blush again. It was so weird to hear Mackenzie talking about me like that, perfect Mackenzie; to think that she'd noticed me, watched me. That she wanted to kiss me, that she'd thought about kissing me. Weird, but not – disgusting or anything.

'And you're the one who's brave.' Mackenzie nudged me. 'Robin Hood.'

'*Me?* Are you kidding? I could never stand up in front of the whole school like you do, I couldn't act in plays and recite poems. I can't talk to strangers like you do. That's brave.'

'No, I'm confident. There's a difference. You've got courage, real courage. You don't care what other people think, you wouldn't let it stop you. *That's* what I don't have.' She snorted suddenly. 'I didn't want to be in that stupid concert. I don't want to perform. I want to *cook*. I don't want to act, and strut all over the stage, but everyone expects me to, and I don't know how to get out of it. So I got Dad to kick up a stink about Charles Le Tan and say I had to go and see him instead. I wasn't brave enough to just say, *no, I don't want to,* this *is what I want to do.* I'm a coward, Jem. And that's why I ran away from you. That's why I ran away tonight.' She searched for my eyes in the dim light. 'But you came after me, you're here now, because you're brave. If it wasn't for you, we wouldn't be sitting here talking. I'd still be pretending everything was okay, that there was nothing going on between us.'

'There isn't anything going on between us,' I said.

Mackenzie said, 'No. But you're still here. *You* haven't run away. So . . .' She hesitated. 'Are you, at least . . . thinking about it?'

'Yeah,' I whispered. 'I'm thinking about it.'

We were both silent then, for what felt like a lifetime.

At last Mackenzie said softly, 'Okay. That's enough for me, for now.'

I could feel my heart banging so hard I was surprised Mackenzie couldn't hear it too. Courage, I thought. If Mackenzie and I were going to be . . . a couple, we were going to need plenty of that. There – I thought it. I let the words run through my mind.

Cautiously I let myself imagine a little more. It would be so good to have a best friend again . . . I imagined touching Mackenzie, kissing her. My heart beat even harder.

I reached over and picked up Mackenzie's hand and held it. Mackenzie drew in a breath, then she moved her thumb softly across the back of my hand. Shivers ran through my whole body.

For a long time we sat there, just holding hands. I felt as if all the electricity that lit up the streets and towers of Sydney was tingling through my blood. The whole world, the entire mysterious universe, had shrunk to this, to the clasp of our two hands. And I realised this was all that mattered, this was the only real thing in all the world; this moment contained the whole world in it. If I were a poet I could write about that.

I said, 'Look at the stars.'

'There aren't as many as there were at Heathersett River.'

'They're still there. We just can't see them.'

'The lights are too bright,' said Mackenzie. 'The stars are invisible.'

'Just because they're invisible doesn't mean they don't exist.'

'If you say so.'

'One day,' I said. 'There will be only light.'

'You remember that?'

'Of course I do. I know it off by heart.'

'*Really?*' Then Mackenzie whispered, 'A season of stars? Forever?'

We sat, holding hands beneath the stars, and our faces turned towards each other, and I wished that the moment could last forever, the moment that held everything in it; when hope multiplied like stars, and anything and everything was possible, before our paths narrowed and divided and carried us away into the future, before any decisions were made or words were said that made us into the people we chose to be; before any promises were made or broken; the moment that was already speeding away from us, the moment before we kissed.

about the author

Kate Constable was born in Melbourne. She spent some of her childhood in Papua New Guinea, without television, but close to a library, where she 'inhaled' stories. She studied Law at uni before realising this was a mistake, then worked in a record company when it was still fun. She left the music industry to write the Chanters of Tremaris trilogy: *The Singer of All Songs*, *The Waterless Sea* and *The Tenth Power*, as well as a stand-alone Tremaris novel, *The Taste of Lightning*. Kate lives in West Preston, Melbourne, with her husband and two daughters.